SUPER TURBO

SAVES THE DAY!

VS. THE FLYING NINJA SQUIRRELS

VS. THE PENCIL POINTER

PROTECTS THE WORLD

By Lee Kirby

Illustrated by George O'Connor

LITTLE SIMON

New York   London   Toronto   Sydney   New Delhi

LITTLE SIMON

An imprint of Simon & Schuster Children's Publishing Division • 1230 Avenue of the Americas, New York, New York 10020 • Copyright © 2017 by Simon & Schuster, Inc. This Little Simon bind-up May 2019. All rights reserved, including the right of reproduction in whole or in part in any form. LITTLE SIMON is a registered trademark of Simon & Schuster, Inc., and associated colophon is a trademark of Simon & Schuster, Inc. For information about special discounts for bulk purchases, please contact Simon & Schuster Special Sales at 1-866-506-1949 or business@simonandschuster.com. The Simon & Schuster Speakers Bureau can bring authors to your live event. For more information or to book an event contact the Simon & Schuster Speakers Bureau at 1-866-248-3049 or visit our website at www.simonspeakers.com. Designed by Jay Colvin. The text of this book was set in Little Simon Gazette.

Manufactured in the United States of America 0419 FFG 10 9 8 7 6 5 4 3 2 1

ISBN 978-1-5344-5635-8

CONTENTS

CONTENTS

1

ALL QUIET IN CLASSROOM C

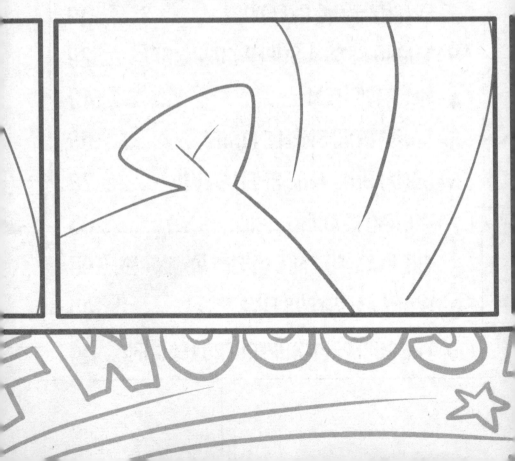

But for now it was perfectly quiet at Sunnyview Elementary. No kids running down the halls, no teachers giving out pop quizzes, no second-grade students reaching into Turbo's cage—

Oh, who's Turbo, you ask? He's this little guy here.

If you couldn't guess, Turbo is a hamster. His fur is mostly white, but he has a big brown spot on his back. He has little pink ears and buck teeth.

And this—er—palace is Turbo's home. Here in the corner of Ms. Beasley's second-grade class.

Turbo, you see, is the official pet of Sunnyview Elementary's Classroom C.

And even on a day like today, when the school was closed for snow, Turbo took his job as classroom pet very seriously.

He made sure to do all his regular classroom pet things.

He drank some water. *GLUG,*
GLUG, GLUG.

He ate some pellets. *MUNCH,*
MUNCH, MUNCH.

And he ran on his hamster wheel.
SQUEAK, SQUEAK, SQUEAK.

When he was finished, only a few

minutes had passed. Now what? Usually Turbo liked when the kids went out to recess and he got some peace and quiet. But today it was almost *too* quiet.

Suddenly, it wasn't quiet anymore. Turbo was sure he heard a rustling coming from the cubbies.

Straining his tiny ears, Turbo listened as hard as he could.

"There is definitely something there," Turbo said to no one in particular. "I'm the official pet of Classroom C, and so it is my duty to find out the source of this mystery sound!"

Finally, Turbo got to where the noise seemed to be coming from. And then he saw a tail and it belonged to a totally terrible, awful, frightening . . .

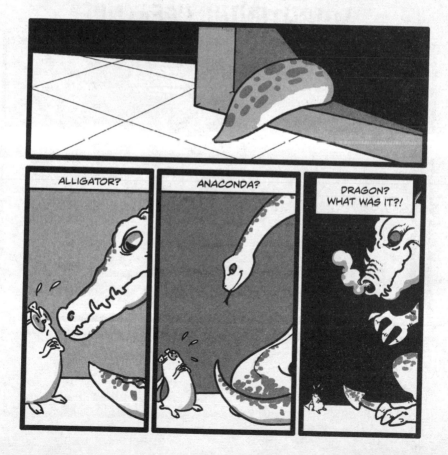

2

THE MOST TERRIBLE, AWFUL, FRIGHTENING CREATURE

Turbo steadied himself and . . .

"Be careful!" yelled the owner of the tail that surely belonged to the most terrible, awful, frightening creature anyone had ever imagined. "If you grab my tail like that, it might break off!"

The strange new visitor turned

to face Turbo. Now that Turbo could get a good look at him, this stranger wasn't quite the most terrible, awful, frightening creature anyone had ever imagined. Unless the person who imagined him was incredibly afraid of small, green-spotted lizards.

"Who are you?" sputtered Turbo.

"I'm Leo," said the small, green-spotted lizard. "I'm from Classroom A. Who are *you*?"

Gasp! Another classroom pet?!

Turbo had always wondered if there were others like him out

there. Turbo stared suspiciously at Leo. Should he reveal his real name?

"What are you doing here in Classroom C?" Turbo decided to ask first.

"I'm here looking for Angelina," replied Leo. "Have you seen her?"

Turbo rubbed his chin. "I don't think so. What does she look like?"

"Well, she's all fuzzy, just like you. And she's got little pink ears, just like you. And she has buck teeth, just like you. Wait . . . are *you* Angelina?"

"Of course not! My name is Turbo," said Turbo. *Oh no!* He had accidentally revealed his real name!

"Oh, well," said Leo, "it didn't hurt to ask. All you fuzzy guys look the same to me."

Suddenly another rustling sound came from the reading nook. Turbo closed his eyes and listened while Leo pulled on a mysterious mask.

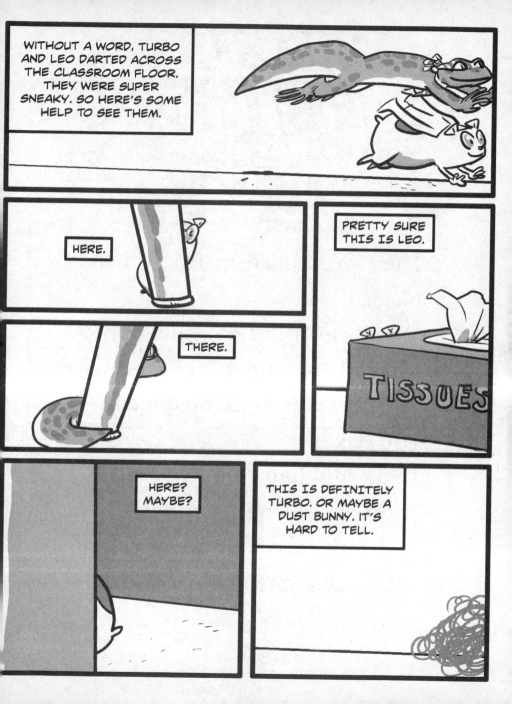

WITHOUT A WORD, TURBO AND LEO DARTED ACROSS THE CLASSROOM FLOOR. THEY WERE SUPER SNEAKY. SO HERE'S SOME HELP TO SEE THEM.

HERE.

THERE.

HERE? MAYBE?

PRETTY SURE THIS IS LEO.

TISSUES

THIS IS DEFINITELY TURBO. OR MAYBE A DUST BUNNY. IT'S HARD TO TELL.

The two stopped in front of the bookcase.

"Nice moves!" Leo said. "They were really . . . *super*."

"Uh, are you wearing a mask?" Turbo asked.

"No," said Leo. "Don't be silly."

Turbo wasn't being silly and he was pretty sure he had seen Leo actually run *up* some *walls*.

Then, on the bookcase, a book lurched out several inches from the shelf. A mysterious figure came into view. It was fuzzy. It had pink ears. It had buck teeth.

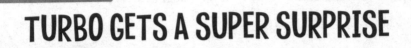

TURBO GETS A SUPER SURPRISE

"Angelina!" cried Leo as he pulled off his mask.

Ah, so this was Angelina. Turbo wondered what she was doing in Classroom C when she said, "Can you help me get this book? I'm tired of all the books in Classroom B. Too many pictures, not enough words."

Another classroom pet?! Turbo was flabbergasted. What a day today was turning out to be!

Angelina started pushing the book farther toward the edge of the shelf. Quick as lightning, Leo raced up the bookcase to help her.

Meanwhile, Turbo ran off to get a pillow to catch the book.

On the count of three, Angelina and Leo gave a big shove, and the book fell right onto the pillow.

Leo skittered down the side of the bookcase, and Angelina simply jumped off the shelf onto the pillow. Now that she was up close, Turbo could see the resemblance.

Turbo shook his head. "I have to admit, I never knew there were any other classroom pets," he said, sort of embarrassed.

"Every classroom has its own pet," explained Angelina. She held out her hand to shake Turbo's.

OUCH!

"But that's not my real super-power," Angelina added.

Superpower? What was going on? But before Turbo could respond, Leo jumped between them.

"Ha-ha, that's enough, Angelina," Leo said quickly. "Okay, well, we'll be getting along. Turbo, it was nice to meet you—"

Suddenly something fluttered onto the floor.

"Hey?" said Turbo. "Is that a . . . mask?"

Leo swiftly scooped up the mask and hid it behind his back.

Turbo rubbed his hand gingerly. "Wow, you're strong!"

"Of course I'm strong!" she said. "I'm a guinea pig and I have super-pig strength!"

Turbo's mouth fell open. "Super-pig strength?" he asked.

He also noticed that she had a perfect white *W* in the middle of her fur.

But Angelina said, "It's too late now, Leo. He knows."

Leo turned around. Turbo wondered if he was about to run away. But when Leo turned *back* around, he was wearing the mask and a

supercool handkerchief with a giant G on it.

Turbo's eyes practically popped out of his head. Angelina was also now wearing a mask and the *W* on her belly almost seemed to be *glowing.*

AND I'M NOT JUST ANGELINA . . . I'M WONDER PIG!

Turbo looked back and forth between the two pets. "You! Guys! Are! Superheroes?!"

Leo nodded. "But this is top secret information, and you must promise to keep it that way," he told Turbo.

Without a word Turbo raced off. Leo and Angelina just looked at each other.

"I guess that was too much for him," said Angelina.

"Well, we are pretty awesome," said Leo.

Suddenly the caped figure leaped back into view.

Now it was Angelina's and Leo's turn to be surprised.

Leo rubbed his eyes. "Another superhero?! This is *great*! Angelina, leave your book here for now. Let's introduce Super Turbo to the team!"

4

MEET THE TEAM!

"Team?" asked Turbo.

Angelina smiled. "There aren't just other classroom *pets*," she said. "There are other pet *superheroes*! I'll show you the way."

The three heroes scampered over to the vent by the door of Classroom C. Angelina lifted the grate off the

vent so
that Turbo
and Leo could get
inside. They followed her down
the length of the duct until they
came to another grate.

"Hiya, Clever!" Leo said with a
wave as he stepped out.

In a cage way above them, a

green parakeet looked down. "Hey, Leo! Hey, Angelina! Who's that with you guys?"

"This is Super Turbo" said Angelina. "He's the pet protector of Classroom C!"

Clever unlocked her cage and flew down to them. The animals all followed Angelina through the vents. They came out into another room, filled with beakers, scales, and microscopes.

"This is the science lab. Warren lives here," explained Angelina.

Clever flew up to a glass case.

HEY, WARREN! WAKE UP! ITS TIME FOR PROFESSOR TURTLE TO STRIKE AGAIN!

Even with the other animals' help, it still took a very long time to get Warren down to the vents.

"I like your visor," Turbo told Warren.

"Thanks," said Warren. "The . . .

wings . . . make . . . me . . . go . . . faster."

Leo placed his hands where his hips would be if geckos indeed had hips.

SOMETHING SMELLS FISHY

PRINCIPAL

Turbo had never been to the principal's office, but he knew from his time in Classroom C that it was a place to be avoided at all costs. Only students who were in the biggest trouble possible went to the principal's office. So what sort of terrifying pet would live there?! The vent in the principal's office was conveniently located right above a shelf. The room was dark as all the animals filed out one by one. Turbo noticed a big cage that was made of wire—like his—and wood.

Suddenly the lights flickered on.

Meanwhile, Angelina had grabbed a rope the pets kept stashed under the garbage can. Like a pro, she swung the rope and lassoed the door handle. Each animal grabbed onto the end, and together they pulled. The doorknob turned . . . and turned . . . and finally . . . CLICK! They pulled the door open.

"Wow!" Turbo exclaimed. He was very impressed.

The animals filed out of the principal's office and into the hallway. Suddenly there was a voice.

But how?

The pets all thought hard.

"I could build a teleporting machine," offered up Warren. "We could teleport Nell out of the fish tank!"

"You can do that?" asked Turbo, shocked.

"Well . . . I never have before," admitted Warren. "But I could try."

"Even if we could teleport Nell down here, she would still need water to breathe," Leo pointed out.

"I have an idea! Wonder Pig, come with me!" Turbo pulled his cape tight and scampered down the hall.

Angelina looked to the others, shrugged,

and ran off after him. The other animals stood around, unsure of what to do.

"So what did you do to end up here in the hallway, Nell?" asked Clever.

Nell flapped a fin, revealing a long, lightning bolt–shaped scar on her side. "It's a long story," she said. "A story for another time."

Just then, everyone stopped talking. A rumbling sound was coming down the hallway. Suddenly Super Turbo came into view. He was rolling along at superspeed in his hamster ball. Wonder Pig was running to catch up with him.

Clever and Frank barely leaped out of the way as Turbo raced toward them, coming to an abrupt stop as he bounced off Warren's hard shell. Dizzily, Turbo hopped out of the Turbomobile. "We can fill my Turbo-mobile with water, and Nell can ride along with us!"

Leo climbed down the wall he had scurried up. "I don't want to rain on your parade, Super Turbo, but there are holes in that hamster ball. The water will leak out."

"Yeah, but Boss Bunny, you have gum on your utility belt, right? We can chew it up and plug the holes," said Turbo.

Frank rubbed his whiskers. "That sounds almost crazy enough to work."

Clever turned to Nell. "Nell, what do you think?"

Nell looked around at the other fish in her tank, then back at Turbo. "I like this guy! He's nuts! Let's do it!"

Working together, the animal superheroes put Super Turbo's plan into action. The classroom pets with buck teeth—and a lot of the animals had them—chewed up the gum. Clever used her beak to stick the chewed-up gum into every

hole. Warren noticed a bottle cap on the ground and calculated that it would take approximately 15.37 bottle caps of water to fill the Turbo-mobile. Leo scampered up the tank

and back down, carefully filling the bottle cap and then dumping the water into the Turbomobile.

Finally, the job was done. While the superpets held the ball steady, Nell leaped out of her tank and did a perfect triple somersault dive into the Turbomobile.

"Fantastic!" Leo clapped.

"Fantastic Fish! That can be your superhero name!" said Turbo excitedly.

"I like it!" said Nell as she swished her tail. "I'm not just Nell . . . I'm Fantastic Fish!"

SOMETHING *ELSE* SMELLS EVIL

They were all there. Super Turbo, Wonder Pig, the Great Gecko, the Green Winger, Professor Turtle, Boss Bunny, and Fantastic Fish. And they were ready to fight evil!

The only problem was ... what evil? The animals looked at one another, all clearly thinking the same thing.

"So . . . ," began Super Turbo.

"Um . . . ," said the Green Winger.

"Well, uh . . . ," added Boss Bunny.

"I'm hungry," said Professor Turtle.

"Great idea!" exclaimed the Great Gecko. "A snack! We're going to need fuel if we're planning to fight evil today."

The rest of the pets eagerly agreed. Then they crawled, scampered, hopped, flew, rolled, and otherwise walked through the doors of the empty Sunnyview Elementary cafeteria.

"Hold it!" Boss Bunny yelled. "I smell something rotten in here."

"Something rotten? Well, the school *is* closed because of the snow," the Great Gecko offered up. "Maybe they didn't have a chance to take out the trash."

Boss Bunny's pink nose twitched. "This isn't rotten garbage. This is a different smell."

"I don't smell anything," said Fantastic Fish. Although, to be fair, she was underwater.

"Yeah, Boss Bunny, how do you know what evil smells like?" asked Professor Turtle.

Suddenly Wonder Pig burst out laughing. "Boss Bunny, I'm pretty sure you're just hungry. We all are!"

The Great Gecko nodded. "Keep that nose to the ground," he told Boss Bunny. "I'm getting a snack!"

The other classroom pets ran off to the pantry, but Super Turbo hung back. Boss Bunny had seemed so sure there was evil afoot, but where? Who? WHAT? Turbo did one last scan of the cafeteria, then ran off to join his new pals.

By the time Super Turbo reached the other classroom pets, the pantry door was already open. The Great Gecko had scurried up the shelves, where he and the Green Winger threw snacks down to the others.

While everyone happily munched on chips, bagels, and crackers shaped oddly like Nell, Super Turbo noticed that Boss Bunny was still standing back, looking troubled. His nose was twitching more than ever. Super Turbo was starting to get the feeling that Boss Bunny was right. And that's when he saw it . . .

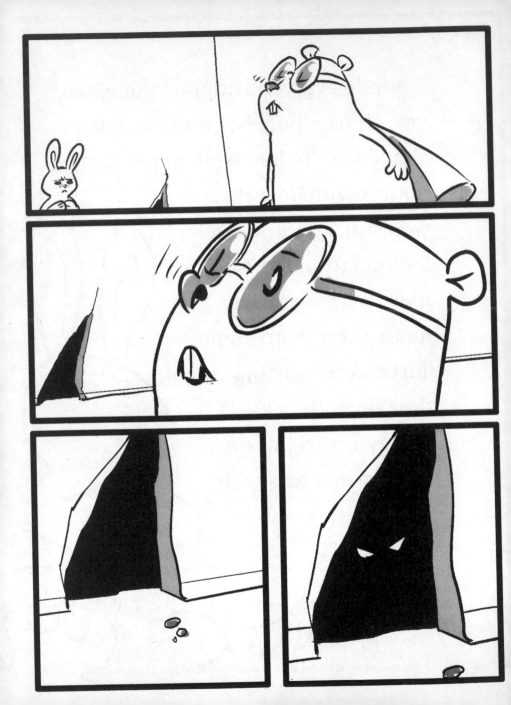

7

WHISKERFACE

A thin pink tail was sticking out of a hole in the wall.

It certainly has been a day for weird tails, Super Turbo thought.

Suddenly the tail disappeared. In its place a pair of beady yellow eyes stared out.

"Well, well, what do we have here?"

said a squeaky voice. A small hairy figure with big ears marched into the pantry.

Super Turbo stepped forward between this stranger and his new friends. He puffed out his chest and adjusted his goggles. "Stay back, Mr., uh . . . ," he paused, not sure what to call this creature.

"Whiskerface!" yelled the stranger.

"Mr. Whiskerface?" asked Turbo.

WHISKERFACE, THE RAT!

I SEE THE PRECIOUS PAMPERED PETS OF SUNNYVIEW ELEMENTARY HAVE FOUND THEIR WAY TO MY SECRET LAIR!

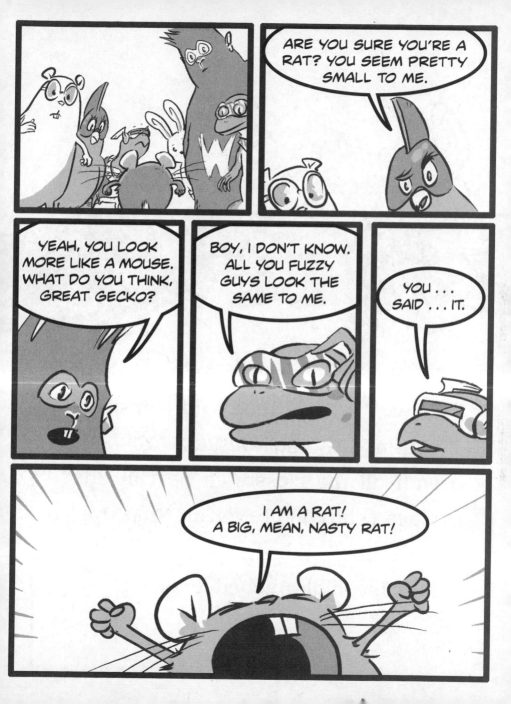

"I've been waiting for you all to arrive," Whiskerface said, sinisterly twirling his long whiskers. "You see, with all the classroom pets in one place, I can capture you and take over the school!" Whiskerface laughed a horrible, high-pitched laugh.

Before the super animals could
respond, Whiskerface cried: "But
wait! There's more! Because after
I take over Sunnyview Elementary, I will use the school as my
base . . . to take over the entire
world!"

The pets blinked.

"I think you may have left out a few steps in that plan of yours," said Fantastic Fish.

"Enough distractions!" Whisker-face yelled. "The point is, I have you all where I want you. And now I will make you my prisoners!"

"Oh yeah?" said Wonder Pig, stepping forward. The *W* on her belly once again seemed to be *glow-ing*. "Well, look around. There's *one* of you and *seven* of us!"

Whiskerface gave a sly grin. "RAT PACK!" he suddenly commanded.

THE PLAN TO TAKE OVER THE WORLD

Through the hole in the wall, a stream of hairy, whiskered, big-eared creatures came pouring into the pantry. In seconds Super Turbo and the other classroom pets were surrounded. Super Turbo tightened his cape. This was it.

In seconds the entire pantry was consumed in an epic battle of good versus evil. Wonder Pig got behind Fantastic Fish and launched the Turbomobile forward. It rolled on a perfect path, scattering Rat Pack-ers like bowling pins. The Great

Gecko scampered back up on the
table, where he and the Green
Winger pelted the rats with grapes
and ketchup packets. Boss Bunny
climbed atop Professor
Turtle's shell and

fought off the Rat Packers with his eraser.

In the chaos Super Turbo saw an opening. He launched himself at Whiskerface and tackled the very

mouse-looking rat off of the bagel he was standing on. The two of them rolled around on the floor. Super Turbo's goggles were fogging up, and it was hard to see. When they cleared, he saw that Whiskerface had been stuffed *into* the bagel during the battle. And the evil rat was now wearing it like a tutu!

But at the same time, the tide had turned against the classroom pets. A group of Rat Packers was rolling the Turbomobile back and forth. Inside the bubble, Fantastic Fish looked like she was seasick.

Professor Turtle had retreated inside his own shell, and a couple of

laughing Rat Packers were playing catch with his visor.

Boss Bunny had been tied up with the string from his own utility belt.

A swarm of Rat Packers had cornered the Green Winger and prevented her from flying.

The Great Gecko had almost escaped by running up a wall, but a Rat Packer got lucky and caught the tip of his tail.

Even Wonder Pig, with her super-pig strength, was captured and down for the count.

Super Turbo suddenly realized that he was the only classroom pet left standing. The fate of his new friends, his school, and perhaps the entire WORLD depended on him!

9

WHEN HAMSTERS FLY!

Super Turbo had to come up with a plan. And fast! He scanned the pantry. The Rat Pack was distracted trying to keep his new friends from escaping. Meanwhile, Whiskerface *was* escaping. And that's when Super Turbo saw it.

Now, you know that a hamster

cannot fly. Maybe if you put a hamster in a catapult or something, you could call that flying. But that's not very nice. But on this day, against these enemies, well . . . guess what? Super Turbo flew!

With a thud, Super Turbo landed atop the table in the pantry. How long before the Rat Pack noticed him? The answer was . . . not long. Already they were racing after him.

Suddenly a lightbulb went on over Super Turbo's head. Well, it didn't go on, but it was there. And there was a long string hanging from it.

Super Turbo took a deep breath. He adjusted his goggles. He fluffed up his cape. And then with all the hamster speed he could muster, he ran as fast as he could to the edge of the table, leaped into the air, and

caught the string that hung from the
lightbulb.

KLANGALANGALANG!

The sound was unbearably loud.

Especially if you happened to be

a tiny little rodent with giant ears. Everyone knows rats hate loud noises! The evil Rat Packers fell down, clutching their ears.

Whiskerface, who was trapped in the bagel tutu, ordered his Rat Pack to cover his ears. But because of the fire alarm, the Rat Pack couldn't hear him. Instead they started crawling back through the hole in the wall. Seeing that he was deserted, Whiskerface turned and ran as well.

As he did, Super Turbo was pretty sure he heard Whiskerface yell, "I'll get you, Super Turbo! This isn't the last you'll see of me!"

THE SUPERPET SUPERHERO LEAGUE!

Later on, in the reading nook in the corner of Classroom C, the new friends gathered to talk about their exciting day.

Angelina turned to Frank. "And I have to say, Frank, you definitely sniffed out that evil before any of us could. It's a good thing we have your super-smelling bunny nose to use from now on."

"Sunnyview is in good hands, thanks to us," said Warren, proudly.

All the pets smiled, content with themselves. All the pets but Leo. He frowned.

"Super!" shouted Clever.

"Pet!" yelled Nell.

"Superhero League!" cried Frank.

"And I propose that Classroom C, right here, be our meeting place," added Angelina.

All the animals agreed it was the perfect place for a team of superhero pets.

○   ○   ○

That night, Turbo returned to his comfy cage in the corner of Classroom C. He carefully folded up his Super Turbo gear and returned it to his secret hiding spot. He looked at

his hamster wheel, his hamster pellets, his water bottle.

Tomorrow, school would be back in session. For all the students, all the teachers, and even Principal Brickford, it would be no different from any other day. But it *would* be different. Because tomorrow, and forever after, Sunnyview Elementary was under the protection of . . .

SUPER TURBO

VS. THE FLYING NINJA SQUIRRELS

By Lee Kirby

Illustrated by George O'Connor

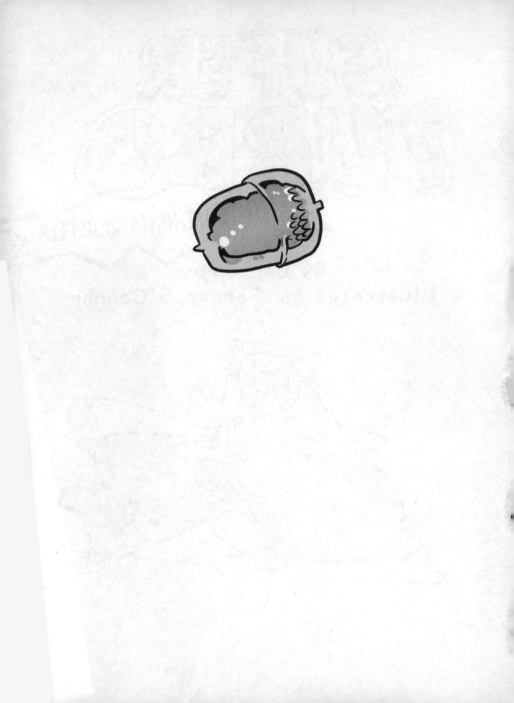

CONTENTS

THE GOLDEN ACORN

Actually, *below* these walls, in the basement. Specifically, in the pantry. Normally, Sunnyview Elementary was filled with kids and teachers and all the things that make up a school. But it was after hours. Everyone was at home or asleep. And not a creature was stirring, except for a— What is that? A mouse?

"Fellow rats!" cried a small, fuzzy creature with huge ears and long whiskers. He addressed a crowd of other creatures just like him. Although he was a bit smaller than

the rest, his whiskers were lon-
ger. This is why he was called . . .
Whiskerface!

"I suppose you're all wondering why I called you here tonight!"
Whiskerface continued.

There was a chorus of whispers.
"Uh, was today Taco Tuesday?"
asked a tiny voice from the back.

"No!" roared Whiskerface. "It's
not even Tuesday. It's Friday!

"As you all know, the Rat Pack recently suffered a defeat at the paws of the pampered pets of Sunnyview Elementary." Whiskerface stroked his whiskers as he reminded his Rat Pack what had happened.

A team of classroom pets had
showed up in his cafeteria and
halted his plan to take over
Sunnyview Elementary and,
eventually, the world!

"But as your fearless leader, I have taken steps to make sure that the Rat Pack won't be defeated again!" Whiskerface cried.

As he said this, a couple of Rat Packers approached Whiskerface's podium, carrying what looked like a box covered with a blanket. The crowd murmured excitedly.

Whiskerface waited for the sounds to die down. "Have you all heard of . . . the Golden Acorn?!"

"Exactly!" yelled Whiskerface. "And according to legend, the Golden Acorn gives great strength and speed to its owner! And I . . ." Whiskerface paused dramatically, looking around the room. "I am now in possession of the Golden Acorn!"

The room buzzed. Everyone wanted to know how Whiskerface had stolen the Golden Acorn.

"I defeated the ninja squirrels in combat," Whiskerface declared, describing the epic battle.

"And now I present to you . . . the Golden Acorn!" Whiskerface cried. He dramatically pulled off the blanket.

The room fell silent. Finally, a voice from the back called out: "Uh . . . , Whiskerface, sir . . . The acorn . . . It's—it's not there."

Whiskerface gasped. "It's gone!"
he screamed. "Someone has stolen
the Golden Acorn . . . again!"

RETURN OF THE SUPERPET SUPERHERO LEAGUE

Meanwhile, in Classroom C of Sunnyview Elementary, Turbo was running his daily laps on his hamster wheel.

Who is Turbo, you ask? Turbo is the official pet of Classroom C. It's a responsibility he takes very seriously. But there is a lot more to Turbo than just that.

You see, Turbo is not just a classroom pet hamster. Turbo is also . . . a superhero! As the heroic Super Turbo, he fights a never-ending battle against evil. And Turbo *himself* recently learned that he is not alone! All the classroom pets of Sunnyview Elementary are superheroes.

Not very long ago, Super Turbo and the other pets had teamed up to prevent Whiskerface and his Rat Pack from taking over the school and then the world! After that, Super Turbo and his friends had decided to fight evil together. And they would fight it as:

THE SUPERPET SUPERHERO LEAGUE!

Turbo was lost in thought when two faces suddenly appeared at his cage.

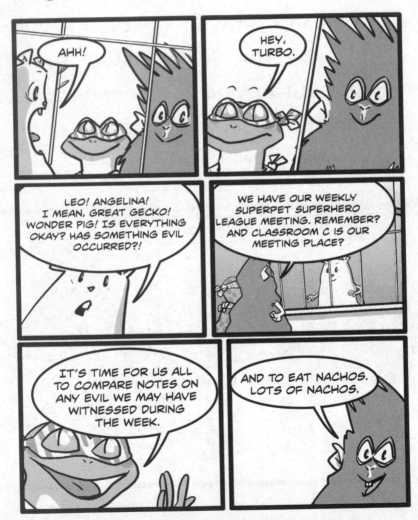

Turbo *hadn't* remembered. But he was excited to see the rest of the team, hear about their solo adventures, and of course, eat some nachos. And it didn't make sense to go to a Superpet Superhero League meeting as plain old Turbo. He would go as . . . Super Turbo!

Super Turbo climbed out of his cage and raced down to the reading nook. That was the meeting place for the Superpet Superhero League.

The Great Gecko and Wonder Pig were already there, of course, and so was Warren, the science lab turtle.

The cover to a vent was resting against the wall. The superpets used the vents as a secret way to travel from room to room in Sunnyview Elementary. Only Wonder Pig, with her amazing maze-running skills, knew where all the vents led.

Suddenly there came a rumbling sound from the vents. Clever, the parakeet from Classroom D—who was also known as the Green Winger—came in, pushing the Turbomobile.

Turbo had generously given his Turbomobile to Nell—also known as Fantastic Fish. That way she could attend meetings and get around the school.

Finally, Frank—also known as Boss Bunny—came hopping in. Now, the superpets were assembled!

The Green Winger thoughtfully took notes as each super-pet detailed their week's adventures. Boss Bunny, the official pet of the principal's office, went first.

Fantastic Fish reported that, from her fish tank in the hallway, she noticed the janitor never locked his closet. That wasn't necessarily evil, but it was something that the superpets could look into.

The Great Gecko mentioned that Classroom A was going on a field trip next Thursday.

Wonder Pig told them how she had snuck into the cafeteria on Taco Tuesday, and that's where she had gotten the nachos. The superpets all clapped for her.

The Green Winger took a break from writing to report that she had witnessed no evil, but had perfected

a brand-new acrobatic routine she was anxious to share with them all.

Super Turbo said that all was safe in Classroom C, though he did note to himself to keep a closer eye on Meredith.

Finally, it was Professor Turtle's turn to speak. Super Turbo leaned back. This would take a while. Everyone loved Professor Turtle, but he *was* a turtle, and sometimes it took him a long time to say things.

Well, that was quick! And almost as quickly, the superpets were headed to the lab!

THINGS GO BOOM!

The superpets raced down the vent, with Professor Turtle leading the way. In fact, Professor Turtle was moving so fast that Super Turbo was having trouble keeping up. Or maybe Super Turbo was moving slower than usual?

Probably shouldn't have had so many nachos, he thought. Then he noticed that Wonder Pig was struggling to keep up alongside him too. And so was Boss Bunny.

The superpets exited the vent onto one of the lab's worktables. A brown papier-mâché mountain was resting on the table before them.

The Great Gecko scampered up the side of the volcano and peered down the hole. "Hey, there's a soda bottle in here!" he exclaimed in surprise.

"Yes!" replied Professor Turtle. "That's where we'll be mixing our own lava! First, we need some water." He glanced at Fantastic Fish.

"Don't look at me," said Fantastic Fish from the Turbomobile. "I need all the water I have."

Super Turbo had an idea. He attached a rubber tube to the end of a faucet, and the Great Gecko ran the other end of the tube to the top of the volcano. Using her super-pig strength, Wonder Pig turned on the faucet to fill the bottle with warm water.

"Now we need to add baking soda!" yelled Professor Turtle.

"We're going to bake a soda?!

Yuck! I prefer my soda cold," said Wonder Pig.

"Not me. I don't even like soda. The bubbles go right up my nose," added Boss Bunny.

"It's too bad someone already emptied this soda bottle if we're going to need to bake it," said the Great Gecko from atop the volcano.

"Are we even allowed to use an oven without supervision?" asked Super Turbo.

Professor Turtle ran over to a box of white powder and stuck in a spoon. "This is baking soda. Green Winger, if you could kindly drop some of this into the volcano?"

The Green Winger flew the baking soda to the top of the volcano. She and the Great Gecko stirred it.

"One final thing!" said Professor Turtle. "Vinegar!"

Wonder Pig and Super Turbo carefully carried a bottle of vinegar up to the top of the volcano. They slowly turned the bottle upside down.

"And now!" yelled Professor Turtle. "Mount Krakabooma erupts!"

Boss Bunny covered his ears. The Green Winger covered her eyes. Fantastic Fish couldn't really cover the Turbomobile. They waited. But nothing happened. And then . . .

"Ha-ha! That was GREAT!" yelled Professor Turtle from on his back.

All the superpets were covered in lava. They agreed they should probably clean up the mess and then head back to their own classrooms to clean up *themselves*.

Just as Super Turbo was about to head back

to Classroom C, a glint of something caught his eye.

"Professor Turtle? What is that in
your cage?" he asked.

"You know, I'm not quite sure,"
said Professor Turtle, removing
his Super Visor. "It's shaped like
an acorn. I found it in the school
cafeteria this morning, and I was
just . . . drawn to it. I've always
liked shiny things."

Super Turbo tried to take a step closer to get a better view, but his paws were stuck to the floor. "Ugh, I better go wash off before I get stuck here forever!" he said. He carefully unstuck each of his paws and scampered down the vent to Classroom C.

AN INVISIBLE VISITOR

Safely back in Classroom C, Turbo took a shower in the drinking fountain. Then he cracked open a window to let the wind dry his fur.

It had certainly been an eventful day, even without evil to fight. Turbo was tired and he deserved a nap. But first, he had to do his patrol of Classroom C.

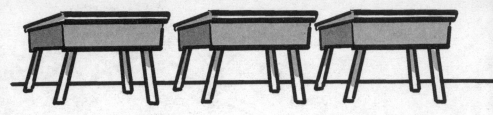

Desks all in a row? Check.

Chalk in the chalkboard holder? Check.

Hamster wheel nice and squeaky? Check.

Supergear safely stashed and drying out? Check.

Well, thought Turbo, clapping his paws together, *looks like it's all clear in Classroom C!*

Turbo pulled out his hammock and settled in. He lay back, and just as his eyes began to close . . .

Turbo sat upright in his hammock. He could have sworn he saw . . . something. A shadow. He scanned the room from his cage. *No, I'm just tired and my eyes are playing tricks on me,* he decided. He lay back down. And then . . .

Again! This time Turbo was sure something was in the classroom with him. He put on his still-damp Super Turbo gear and climbed down from his cage.

Using all of his super-hamster sneakiness, Super Turbo searched the classroom.

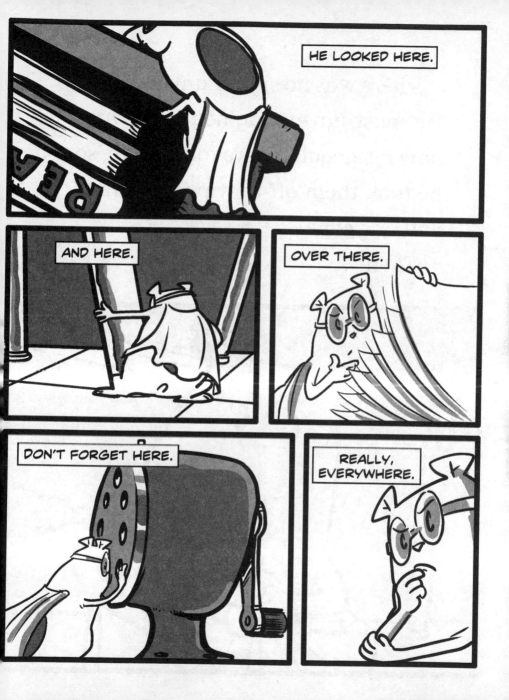

There was no sign of any intruder. He must have imagined it all. And now his goggles were fogging up, so he took them off to wipe the lenses with his cape.

Then . . .

What had just happened?! Super
Turbo raced over to the door. He
certainly couldn't open it himself.
But he was sure that someone—or
something—had just gone out it.

"This looks like a bigger mystery
than any *one* superhero can solve!"
Turbo announced.

He ran over to the vents that connected all the superpets' classrooms
to one another. He grabbed the ruler
that lay just inside the vent.

When they had formed the Super-pet Superhero League, the Great Gecko had come up with a secret code the superpets could use to communicate through the vents. Super Turbo tapped the corner of the ruler on the metal floor of the vent. The sound echoed throughout the whole system.

One tap meant: *All's well, nothing to worry about here. Carry on.*

Two taps meant: *Hey, I'm hungry. Who wants to go to the cafeteria for some snacks?*

And three? Three taps meant:

5

SUPERPETS ON PATROL

The Superpets quickly arrived at Classroom C, ready to fight evil. Surprisingly, Professor Turtle had been first to arrive. He was usually the last, since he moved so slowly. The rest of the team followed him in.

"I'd just emptied out the Turbomobile when I heard the call," said Fantastic Fish.

"What's happening, Super Turbo?"
asked Wonder Pig. "When I heard
the first tap, I was like, oh good, all
is well. But then I heard the second
tap and I was like, Super Turbo is
hungry? We just had nachos! And
then I heard the third tap . . ."

"Well, I don't know if it's evil, but something very strange is definitely going on," said Super Turbo. He told the Superpet Superhero League what he had seen . . . or rather, *not* seen.

The Great Gecko stroked his chin. "You were right to sound the alarm, Super Turbo. This is very strange indeed."

"I wonder if the intruder was invisible?" asked Fantastic Fish.

"Or what if it was a g-g-ghost?" stammered Boss Bunny.

The Great Gecko was about to speak again when Professor Turtle said, "The smartest idea will be for us to split up into smaller teams and

the hallways. Green Winger: you and Boss Bunny can check the gymnasium. Super Turbo: you and I will cover the cafeteria. Let's go, superpets!"

Everyone was so surprised by Professor Turtle's quick thinking and take-charge attitude that they stood still for a second. But it *was* a good plan, so they sprang into action.

explore the school. We can cover more ground that way and meet back here in thirty minutes."

The Great Gecko blinked. "Yeah, what Professor Turtle said."

"Okay!" continued Professor Turtle. "Great Gecko: you, Wonder Pig, and Fantastic Fish can check

Fantastic Fish knew the hallways the best, so it made a lot of sense for her to cover them. With the Great Gecko and Wonder Pig alongside, they were able to finish their patrol in no time. They didn't see any sign of the invisible intruder, but they did stop to lock the janitor's closet.

Boss Bunny and the Green Winger arrived in the gymnasium. Using his bunny-burrowing powers, Boss Bunny squeezed behind the bleachers to see if there was any sign of the intruder.

The Green Winger flew up to the ceiling to see if a bird's-eye view revealed some evil. They didn't find anything.

Since they had extra time, and all the extra space, the Green Winger decided to show off the new acrobatic move she had perfected: the Triple Loop-de-Loop with an Aerial Twist.

"Brava!" Boss Bunny clapped.

Meanwhile, Super Turbo and Professor Turtle were in the cafeteria. Once again, Super Turbo found he was having a hard time keeping up with Professor Turtle. But now Super Turbo was pretty sure that he wasn't getting *slower*. Professor Turtle was definitely getting *faster*. He seemed to be growing more confident, too. It was like a whole new professor!

The first time Super Turbo had been to the cafeteria was also when he'd had his first clash with evil. He and the superpets had battled Whiskerface and his Rat Pack. There hadn't been a peep from those rodent rascals since then, but Turbo gave a shudder at what a close call their battle had been. And hadn't something else happened recently in the cafeteria too?

The two superheroes completed their sweep of the cafeteria and came up empty-pawed. Nothing suspicious to be found! They headed back to meet up with the others at Classroom C.

A few moments later, two sets of beady yellow eyes peered out of a tiny crack in the cafeteria wall.

"Did you hear that? The turtle found the Golden Acorn!"

"Whiskerface is going to be so pleased when we tell him!"

THIS FIGHT IS TOTALLY NUTS

Back in their meeting spot in the reading nook of Classroom C, the superpets all shared what they found—or rather, didn't find—on their patrols.

Super Turbo walked away from the group and wondered to himself: *Did I actually see anything? Was that really the door opening and*

closing that I heard? Or was it all in my head?

Just then, something rattled. It was the doorknob. "Guys! Look!" Super Turbo yelled, pointing.

The superpets froze as the doorknob turned, and the door slowly opened.

"Oh my gosh, they *are* invisible!" yelled Wonder Pig, and she began karate chopping the air all around her.

"They're g-g-ghosts!" shrieked Boss Bunny, and fainted into the Great Gecko's arms.

"Shh! Be quiet and hide!" said Super Turbo.

The superpets all found hiding spots in the bookshelf and waited.

After a few moments, a masked figure dressed all in black crept into the room. It didn't make a noise. It had a huge bushy tail. And it was followed by two identical figures.

Suddenly, Professor Turtle yelled out: "NINJA SQUIRRELS!"

The three Ninja Squirrels snapped to attention and took battle stances.

Their cover blown, the superpets leaped out into their best super-hero poses. Suddenly, the Ninja Squirrels launched themselves at the superpets.

"They're not just Ninja Squirrels!" the Green Winger yelled. "They're FLYING Ninja Squirrels!"

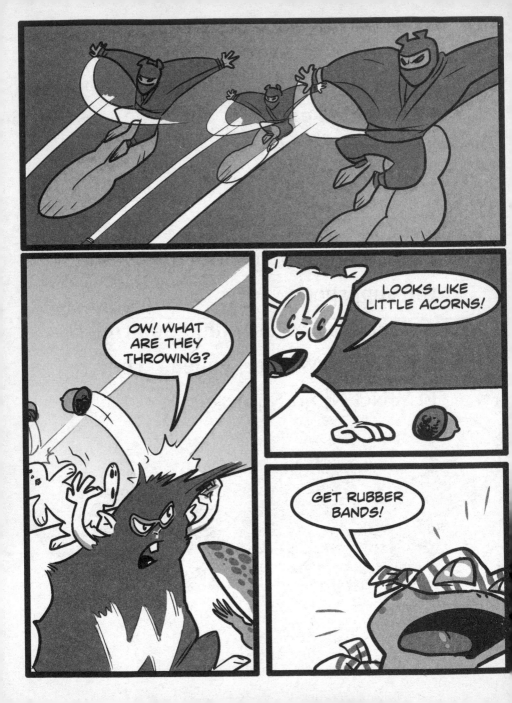

The Green Winger flapped into the air as the rest of the superpets dove out of the way of the Flying Ninja Squirrels.

With her supercool Triple Loop-de-Loop with an Aerial Twist maneuver, she was able to make two of the Flying Ninja Squirrels crash into each other.

But on the ground, the squirrels were almost too quick for the eye to follow.

Even the Great Gecko, one of the speedier members of the Superpet Superhero League, was having a hard time keeping up with the acrobatic Flying Squirrels. Surprisingly, Professor Turtle, whose normal fighting technique was to curl up into his shell, was doing quite well.

The battle raged around Classroom C. Super Turbo climbed up on top of his cage and saw that the room—*his* room!—was getting destroyed! And what sort of official classroom pet would he be if he let that happen?

EVERYBODY STOP!

7

EVERYBODY STOPS

Everyone stopped and looked at Super Turbo.

"This is my classroom," he said. "And you all are really making a mess of it."

The rest of the animals hung their heads, embarrassed.

"We're sorry, Super Turbo," said Wonder Pig. Then she strolled up to the nearest Flying Ninja Squirrel, held out her hand, and said, "Hi, I'm Wonder Pig. Nice to meetcha."

The Flying Ninja Squirrel glanced back to her friends, shrugged, and held out her paw. "I'm Nutkin."

The rest of the superpets and

Flying Ninja Squirrels made introductions to one another. Super Turbo was surprised at how polite the ninjas were. They didn't seem so evil, after all.

"So what brings you to Sunnyview Elementary, Nutkin?" Super Turbo asked.

"We are missing something," said Nutkin after a slight pause. "Something very important to us. And we have reason to believe it is somewhere in this school."

"What are you missing?" asked the Great Gecko.

Nutkin looked back and forth to

the other Flying Ninja Squirrels. "This is a very, uh, delicate matter for us. Do you mind if we take a moment to discuss?"

"Take your time," said the Great Gecko, waving his hand. "We have some important matters to discuss as well."

The two groups moved to opposite sides of Classroom C and formed huddles.

After a few minutes, the Flying Ninja Squirrels signaled that they were ready.

"We can tell from our battle that you are honorable opponents," said Nutkin. "And because we feel we can trust you, we will tell you what we are missing. It is the sacred symbol of our clan, and we believe it gives great strength and speed to its owner. It is . . . the Golden Acorn!"

Super Turbo shot a surprised look at Professor Turtle.

"Weeeell," Professor Turtle said slowly, "I think I know where you can find that."

SUNNYVIEW ELEMENTARY

The Superpet Superhero League and the Flying Ninja Squirrels followed Professor Turtle down the vent to the science lab. Maybe it was because Professor Turtle didn't want to give up the Golden Acorn, or maybe he was just tired after their epic battle, but it was the first time all day that Super Turbo had no trouble keeping up with him.

They exited the vent next to the professor's terrarium. Professor Turtle slowly walked up to the cage and let out a gasp.

8

WHISKERFACE WINS!

The superpets and Ninja Squirrels stared at the place where the Golden Acorn *should* have been. Suddenly, a familiar and very squeaky voice rang out. "That's right! Your precious Golden Acorn is gone!" said Whiskerface, strolling into view. "I have it!"

"Whiskerface! You rat!" yelled Super Turbo.

"Hey, Nutkin, look! It's the gold-polish salesman!" said one of the Flying Ninja Squirrels. "That's the guy who stole the Golden Acorn!"

"Gold-polish salesman?" asked a Rat Packer in the back.

"Yeah, he asked to see the Golden

Acorn so that he could demonstrate his polish. We showed it to him, and he ran off with it, all the way back to the school," said the other Flying Ninja Squirrel.

"Hey, you told us you defeated the Ninjas in combat . . . ," said another Rat Packer.

"Never mind what the ninny Ninja Squirrels say!" squeaked Whiskerface, his whiskers trembling. "All that matters is that I got the Golden Acorn!"

"And then you *lost* the Golden Acorn," Professor Turtle pointed out.

"Yes, and then I *lost* the Golden Acorn," Whiskerface said through gritted teeth. "But then I *got* the Golden Acorn again! And now that I have it, I will be *unstoppable*!"

"You're nuts!" said Fantastic Fish from within the Turbomobile. "First off, your plan is missing some key steps *again*. Second, do you really believe that acorn is going to give you superpowers?"

"Just ask your new buddies, the Flying Pinhead Squirrels! Or better yet, your old pal Professor Turtle!" Whiskerface squealed.

Super Turbo saw Professor Turtle look sadly down at the ground. Maybe his strength and speed *were* all because of the Acorn. . . .

Suddenly, Super Turbo had an idea. "Yeah, well, that's not what I heard," he said. The Flying Ninja Squirrels, the superpets, and the Rat Packers all looked at him.

"That's not what you heard, huh?" sneered Whiskerface. "Well, why don't you tell me what you heard?"

"Well," said Super Turbo, turning to face Nutkin and her squirrels. "You guys told me how you had to get the Golden Acorn back before it's too late. Before it does any more *damage*. . . ." Super Turbo winked at Nutkin.

"Damage?" squeaked Whisker-face. "What do you mean? What kind of damage?"

Nutkin stepped forward. "It's true that the Golden Acorn gives strength and speed to whoever owns it. But unless you know the secret word to unlock it, the acorn will do the absolute opposite. It will suck out any powers you already have!"

"You're—you're—you're lying!" cried Whiskerface.

Just then, Professor Turtle started to wobble.

The Great Gecko ran up to Professor Turtle. "I can't believe it!" he said. "Professor Turtle has been drained of all his powers!"

"Oh no!" cried the Green Winger. "Who knows what will happen next!"

9

WHAT? NO, HE DOESN'T!

Whiskerface stared wide-eyed at Professor Turtle.

"You know what?" Whiskerface squeaked. "I don't want this anyway!" He shoved the Golden Acorn into the hands of the Rat Packer next to him and then ran off.

The Rat Packer squeaked in terror and passed the acorn to the rat next

to him. The game of hot potato continued until, finally, one rat handed
the Golden Acorn to Super Turbo.

Then all the Rat Packers ran
screaming from the lab.

"I believe this belongs to you," said
Super Turbo, passing the Golden
Acorn to Nutkin.

Nutkin smiled. "I knew we were right to trust you superpets."

"Are ... they ... gone ... yet?" asked Professor Turtle from the floor.

"That was an impressive display of acting!" said Wonder Pig as she and the Great Gecko turned Professor Turtle right-side up.

Professor Turtle answered as slowly as ever.

The superpets and the Flying Ninja Squirrels made their way back to Classroom C. Professor Turtle was really bringing up the rear now, and Super Turbo hung back to walk with him.

"I guess . . . it really was the . . . acorn that . . . made me . . . so fast," Professor Turtle said sadly. "It was nice . . . while it lasted . . . but I guess I'm back . . . to slowpoke Warren."

"But you're not just slowpoke Warren!" Turbo said. "You're a member of the Superpet Superhero League! And whenever you put on your Super Visor, you're never just Warren . . .

Back in Classroom C, the Flying Ninja Squirrels stood in front of the same open window they had snuck in through.

"Superpets," said Nutkin, "the clan of the Flying Ninja Squirrels will forever be in your debt. You returned our sacred symbol, the Golden Acorn. If you ever need our help, just ask. We live in the big oak tree on the playground."

And with that, the three Flying Ninja Squirrels flew out the window.

"Today was a great day!" said Super Turbo.

"Yeah, it was," said Fantastic Fish.

"We had nachos!" cried Wonder Pig.

"We made a volcano!" exclaimed Boss Bunny.

"We had the best battle ever *and* made some new friends!" said the Great Gecko.

"And I got to be fast . . . for a little while," added Professor Turtle, smiling.

"But, best of all, we defeated evil! Again!" yelled Super Turbo.

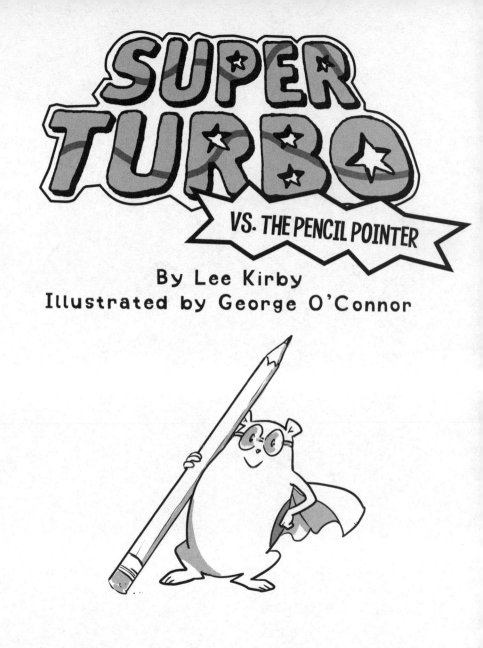

SUPER TURBO
VS. THE PENCIL POINTER

By Lee Kirby

Illustrated by George O'Connor

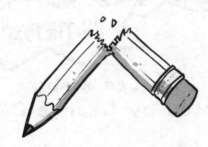

CONTENTS

A VISITOR IN CLASSROOM C

BEHOLD! SUNNYVIEW ELEMENTARY SCHOOL! INSIDE THESE WALLS THERE IS A BIG SECRET!

SUNNYVIEW ELEMENTARY

What is this big secret, you might ask? We'll get to that. For now, Sunnyview Elementary School is just your typical old elementary school. And Classroom C of Sunnyview Elementary School is just your typical second-grade classroom.

Oh sure, Turbo might *look* like an ordinary hamster. But remember that big secret? Well, here it is. You see, Turbo *isn't* an ordinary hamster. He's also . . . Super Turbo, the mightiest super-hamster in the entire known universe!

But the students of Classroom C have no idea that Turbo is a super-hamster. And Turbo has to protect his secret identity. So around the kids, Turbo is just typical Turbo. That's okay with him because being the official pet of Classroom C is a big duty and even superheroes enjoy some time off!

RING-A-DING-DING!

The bell sounded the end of the school day. Some of the students filed past Turbo's cage and waved to him on their way out.

Ms. Beasley spent a few minutes gathering up her things, and then she left too. "Good night, Turbo, see you tomorrow!" she

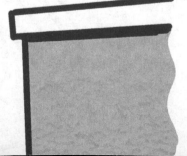

called as she shut the door behind her.

What to do? thought Turbo. He didn't have any plans tonight since there was no Superpet Superhero League meeting on the schedule.

WHAT'S THAT, YOU SAY? YOU'VE NEVER HEARD OF THE SUPERPET SUPERHERO LEAGUE? YOU'VE NEVER HEARD OF THE GREAT GECKO? WONDER PIG? THE GREEN WINGER? BOSS BUNNY? FANTASTIC FISH? NOT EVEN PROFESSOR TURTLE?!

Well then, read closely! You see, Turbo wasn't the only superhero pet in Sunnyview Elementary. The truth is, *all* the class pets were secretly superheroes. And as superheroes, they decided to band together as the Superpet Superhero League to stop evil in and out of the classrooms!

Turbo thought for another

moment about his plans. Suddenly, he knew what he was going to do for the rest of the night. He climbed onto his water bottle and gently lifted the top of his cage. Then he swung down from the table and scurried across the floor to the reading nook. He'd been reading a Rider Woofson adventure the past few nights and he was anxious to see how it ended.

Turbo settled in and was leisurely reading when . . .

CLICK!

What was that noise?

CREAK!

Turbo looked toward the door. Oh no! It was opening! Which meant . . . someone was about to enter Classroom C!

Turbo looked around for a hiding spot.

A foot entered the classroom. Turbo dove underneath his book, hoping it would cover him.

Then he had a horrible thought— what if whoever it was noticed that Turbo wasn't in his cage? *They'll think I've been kidnapped! They'll send out search parties!*

Turbo dared to peek out of his hiding place. He breathed a sigh of relief when he saw that the mysterious visitor was just the school janitor. He was probably coming to empty the trash.

But wait! He wasn't heading for the trash! He was heading directly for Turbo's cage!

OH NO! HE'S ALREADY NOTICED I'M GONE! HE MUST HAVE THE CAGE BUGGED!

The janitor stood in front of Turbo's cage. Then he opened his

supply kit and pulled something
out. What was it? Turbo strained his
eyes but it was too far away to see.

Suddenly there came an awful

high-pitched
drilling sound.

It was almost as awful and high-
pitched as the alarm in the cafeteria, which Turbo had set off one time
in order to defeat an evil rat named
Whiskerface.

And then it was over. The janitor
packed up his things and headed
for the door. He flicked off the lights
as he left.

Phew! That was a close call! thought Turbo. *I better get back to my cage before anyone actually notices I'm gone.*

It took Turbo a while to get back in the dark, and when he finally did, he was relieved to see that everything looked normal. But . . . if everything looked normal, then what was the janitor doing?

THE BIG REVEAL!

Turbo opened his eyes. Sunlight was
streaming in through the classroom
windows. He got up, yawned, and
stretched. Had last night been all
a dream? Turbo looked around. On
the shelf above his cage, he could
see . . . *something.* So it hadn't been
a dream. Whatever the janitor had

installed last night was up there, but Turbo sure couldn't tell what it was.

Was it a machine that shot out laser nets any time a kid picked his nose? Or a freeze ray if someone whispered in class? Or a top secret ghost detector? The possibilities were endless!

Turbo was just about to climb up onto his water bottle and take a closer look when . . .

RING-A-DING-DING!

Students began to file into Classroom C. Turbo would have to wait until later to see what was up there.

Ms. Beasley was making an announcement at the head of the classroom.

Oh good, thought Turbo, she knows all about the mysterious device! She's probably going to warn the kids to stay clear until it can be properly removed from the shelf above my hamster cage.

"Class, I just wanted to point out," Ms. Beasley was saying, "that we have an exciting new addition to the classroom!" She gestured toward Turbo's cage. "A brand-new electric pencil sharpener!" she announced.

The class *oohed* and *aahed* as if Ms. Beasley had just revealed that it was a flying chocolate-maker.

A hand shot up. It was a girl named Meredith whom Turbo had been keeping an eye on. The word in the Superpet Superhero League was that she was a potential troublemaker.

"Ms. Beasley, may I sharpen my pencil?" Meredith asked.

"Yes, Meredith," Ms. Beasley replied. "Anytime anyone needs to sharpen their pencil, they may get up and do so quietly."

Meredith sprang up and ran to the sharpener.

It was awful. Turbo would have covered his ears, but with Meredith right there, all the kids would've probably noticed, and then they'd start asking questions, and then he'd have to reveal his secret identity, and then . . . it was too risky.

Meredith pulled her pencil out of the sharpener and held it up. "Pointy!" she proclaimed.

Pretty soon, the whole class had lined up to sharpen their pencils.

Why is everyone so excited about a pencil sharpener? thought Turbo. *Can't they just chew their pencils into points, like I can?*

Turbo never got his answer. Instead, the pencil sharpening continued. NONSTOP. ALL DAY.

Turbo sat grumpily in his cage, food pellets in his ears to block out the noise. But toward the end of the day, Turbo began to notice something. And that something was falling into his cage. It looked like his cedar chips, but it was lighter and fluffier.

Then Turbo let out a gasp. It was pencil shavings!

The pencil sharpener was dropping pencil shavings into Turbo's cage! Every time a kid sharpened their pencil, a few more flakes fell down! At this rate Turbo was surely going to be buried!

EMERGENCY MEETING!

"I suppose you're all wondering why I called this emergency meeting of the Superpet Superhero League," said Super Turbo.

School had let out a few hours ago. Now the class pets were gathered in their secret meeting place, the reading nook of Classroom C.

Super Turbo brushed a few pencil shavings off his cape. "Something strange is happening in Classroom C," he continued.

"That's funny," said a parakeet named Clever, who was also known as the Green Winger. "Something strange is happening in Classroom D as well!"

"Weird," said Leo, the official pet of Classroom A, also known as the Great Gecko. "I was going to report strange happenings in my

classroom as well!"

"Me too!" exclaimed Angelina the guinea pig, who also known as Wonder Pig. She was the official pet of Classroom B.

"This . . . is . . . mysterious . . . ," Warren said as slowly as you'd expect a turtle to speak. He was the class pet of the science lab, and he was also known as Professor Turtle.

"What's going on?" asked Nell from within the water-filled Turbo-mobile that served as her home when she wasn't in her fish tank. She was also known as Fantastic Fish.

"Hmm ...," said Frank, also known as Boss Bunny. He was the official pet of the principal's office. "And you're telling me this happened in every classroom last night?"

The Green Winger, Wonder Pig, and the Great Gecko all nodded.

"How could the janitor be so care-less?" asked Super Turbo.

"What if . . . ," began Boss Bunny,
"what if the janitor *wasn't* being
careless?"

"Hold on. Who—or *what*—is the *Pencil Pointer*?" asked Fantastic Fish, scratching her head with her fin.

"I think you'd better come with me," said Boss Bunny darkly. "There's something you all need to see."

A POINTY PLAN

The superpets followed Boss Bunny to the vent in Classroom C.

Using her super-pig strength, Wonder Pig removed the vent cover and the animals filed inside.

When the Superpet Superhero League had formed, they'd decided that the best way to travel in secret

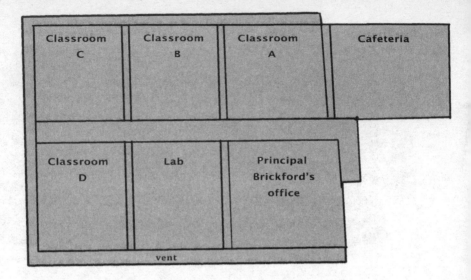

was to use the vent system. It was also their way of communicating. Each pet had an object that they hid just inside the vent in their classroom. They'd tap it on the vent floor, and the sound would echo throughout the whole system. Turbo's object was that ruler right there.

Being a guinea pig, Wonder Pig not only had strength, but also super maze-running abilities. The superpets followed her as she raced through the vents. She popped out into each classroom to make sure that, yes, the Pencil Pointer had indeed struck each and every one!

Now the Superpets climbed out of the vent that led into Principal Baxter Brickford's office.

"It's over here," said Boss Bunny, taking the lead. "On Principal Brickford's desk." He led all the animals to a yellow notepad.

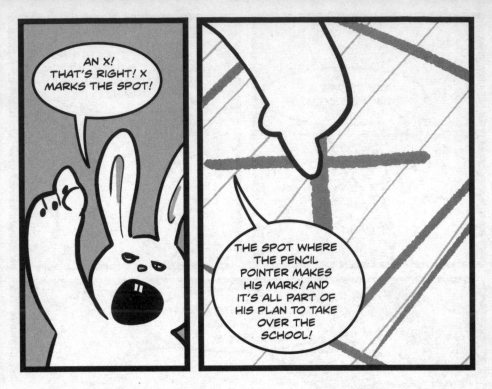

"Boss Bunny, you're sounding a little like our old enemy Whisker-face," said Fantastic Fish. "How does installing a pencil sharpener in each classroom help the Pencil Pointer take over the school?"

"Excellent question!" said Boss Bunny. "First, have you noticed how the kids are mesmerized by these pencil sharpeners?"

"Yes!" exclaimed Super Turbo. "Is it mind control?"

"It very well could be, Super Turbo," said Boss Bunny. "These kids keep sharpening and sharpening and SHARPENING their pencils—"

The Great Gecko snapped his fingers. "Until we're all buried beneath a mountain of pencil shavings!"

"And then there are no superpets to protect the school!" cried Wonder Pig with a gasp.

"Exactly," replied Boss Bunny. "We can't expect the kids and teachers to understand the danger they're in. And with no superpets around, the Pencil Pointer will easily take control of Sunnyview

Elementary School!"

"But *who* is the Pencil Pointer?" asked Wonder Pig, scratching her head. "Is it Principal Brickford?"

"It can't be," said the Green Winger, pointing at the drawings of Boss Bunny. "The Pencil Pointer wants to get *rid* of the school pets, and Principal Brickford clearly loves Frank."

Boss Bunny giggled with delight, then got serious. "It must be someone *above* Principal Brickford! Someone who hates cute, fuzzy animals!"

The Great Gecko leaned forward. "What does it say there toward the bottom of the map?"

Trial in Cafeteria

Super Turbo adjusted his goggles. "It says 'trial in cafeteria.'"

"Well . . . that's . . . mysterious" said Professor Turtle.

"Are you guys thinking what I'm thinking?" asked Wonder Pig.

SNACKS!

SNACK ATTACK!

The Superpet Superhero League arrived at the school cafeteria.

"I know we came here for snacks, but maybe we'll find some clues about this mysterious Pencil Pointer too," said Turbo.

"And maybe we'll find some nacho cheese potato chips!" said

Wonder Pig, licking her lips.

"And some gummy worms!" said the Green Winger. "Way better than real worms!" she added. "Believe me, I would know!"

In the pantry the Great Gecko used his sticky hands and feet and

his super climbing power to scale
the side of the cabinet where the
snacks were kept.

The superpets looked around. The Great Gecko was right. The snack cupboard was completely bare!

"Maybe check the fridge?" called out Fantastic Fish.

"Good idea!" yelled the Great Gecko. He scurried over to the fridge.

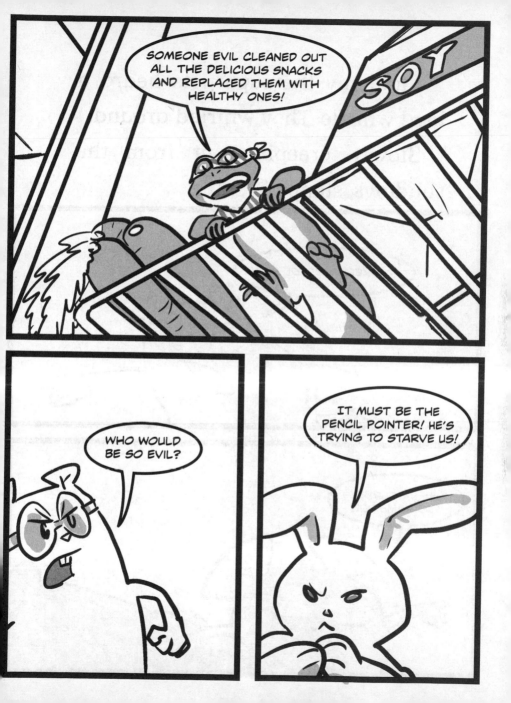

Suddenly the superpets heard a loud whistle. They whirled around.

Slowly, creeping out from the shadows, stepped . . .

"What—what do you have there?" Fantastic Fish stammered, practically drooling with hunger.

"Oh, this?" asked Whiskerface, stroking his long whiskers. "This is just a bag of incredibly delicious nacho cheese potato chips. The *last* bag of incredibly delicious nacho cheese potato chips in the whole school. And maybe even in the whole world!"

CAFETERIA SHOWDOWN

Whiskerface paced back and forth, showing off his goods. "You super*pests* shouldn't even bother looking for the good snacks. My Rat Packers cleaned out the whole cupboard!" He laughed his evil squeaky laugh.

"I can't . . . believe . . . it!" said

Professor Turtle. "Whiskerface . . . is the . . . Pencil Pointer!"

"But now you've taken our snacks!" said Wonder Pig, cracking her knuckles. "Now you've gone too far!"

Whiskerface stood there blinking his beady eyes. "Yeah, sure, I'm totally the, uh, Pointy Pencil guy. You got me."

"Wait, guys!" cried Super Turbo, leaping forward. "Remember what it said on the map? 'Trial in cafeteria'?"

"Yeah . . . that surely was . . . mysterious," said Professor Turtle.

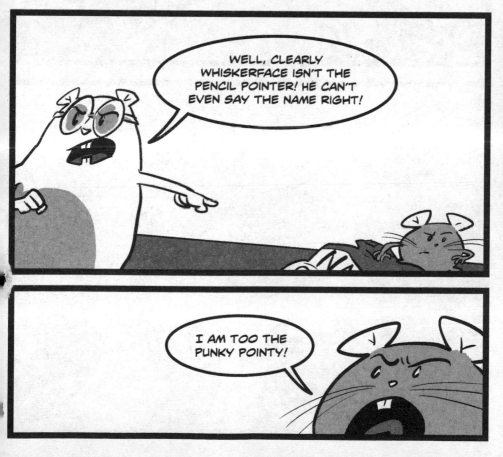

"I don't know what you pooper-pets are talking about," said Whiskerface. "But I think you're all crazy." He started to back away. "You've not heard the last of the Pinky Pusher!" he cried as he dove through the hole in the wall that led to his lair.

The superpets approached the bag of potato chips Whiskerface had left behind.

"Is there anything in there?" asked Super Turbo. "Are they . . . "

Professor Turtle
looked up sadly.
"Gone."

With a sob, Boss
Bunny threw himself
onto his belly, shoveling
pawfuls of potato chip dust into his
mouth.

Wonder Pig and the Great Gecko
grabbed him by the arms and

dragged him away. "It's okay, Boss Bunny. Let it go. Just let it go."

Super Turbo clenched his fists. Whoever this Pencil Pointer was, he was going to pay!

SUPERPETS VS. THE PENCIL POINTER

The superpets sadly made their way back to Classroom C. Super Turbo was pretty sure he could even hear Boss Bunny sniffling a little.

As the pets exited the vent into the classroom, Super Turbo looked up at the pencil sharpener. It was just sitting there, above his cage.

Staring at him. It almost looked like it was . . . smiling?

Using every last bit of his super-hamster speed, Super Turbo bounded up to his cage. With a mighty leap, he practically flew up to the shelf where the pencil sharpener was bolted. But he didn't have enough strength to pull himself up!

He was starting to lose his grip!

"Come on, guys!" shouted the Great Gecko, springing into action. "We have to get up there and help Super Turbo!" Then he looked around. "Well, those of us who *can* actually get up there."

The Great Gecko scampered up the wall while the Green Winger flew over to the shelf. The other animals cheered them on from below.

They each grabbed one of Super Turbo's arms and pulled him onto the shelf. Together, the trio tried to knock the pencil sharpener out of place.

"It's bolted down tight!" grunted Super Turbo. "We need more force!"

BOSS BUNNY! DO YOU HAVE ANYTHING IN YOUR UTILITY BELT THAT WILL TAKE CARE OF THESE SCREWS?

8

ONE DOWN

Super Turbo, Wonder Pig, and the Great Gecko made their way down from the shelf. Then they lay on the floor, exhausted. They had defeated the pencil sharpener, but it had taken everything they had. And there were still plenty more sharpeners out there!

Fantastic Fish, Boss Bunny,

Professor Turtle, and the Green Winger came over to check on them.

"Are you all right?" Fantastic Fish asked Super Turbo. Super Turbo gave a thumbs-up. The Great Gecko managed to nod. And the Green Winger waved a wing.

"Good," said Fantastic Fish. "You guys really sent that pencil sharpener flying!"

"It was . . . awesome!" Professor Turtle cried.

"Nice work," Boss Bunny agreed.

"Definitely," said the Green Winger. "But we should probably go make sure nothing got broken."

The superpets made their way over to the reading nook, where the pencil sharpener had landed.

"Looks like the pencil sharpener is still in one piece," noted Fantastic Fish.

Super Turbo nodded. A few books had gotten knocked over and there were pencil shavings scattered about, but there was no other damage.

Then Super Turbo noticed something else. It was a piece of paper that seemed to have fallen onto the floor.

A REALLY POINTY PENCIL?

Super Turbo looked down at the drawing. He suddenly felt really guilty. The kids of Classroom C had been *so* excited about the pencil sharpener.

"Guys, what if this *wasn't* some sinister plan crafted by the mysterious Pencil Pointer?"

Super Turbo and the superpets knew what they had to do. They cleaned up the reading nook. Then they worked together to get the pencil sharpener up on Ms. Beasley's desk so she'd see it first thing when she came in.

Their job done, the superpets made their way to the vent so they could return to their respective classrooms.

As he left, Boss Bunny turned back to Super Turbo. "Just one more thing," he said. "If the Pencil Pointer isn't real, then what is that map I showed you guys? And what does 'trial in the cafeteria' mean?"

Super Turbo shook his head. "I don't know, Boss Bunny. But right now, I think we all need some rest." And with that, Super Turbo climbed into his cage and fell into a deep sleep.

AND IT WAS ALL WORTH IT

The next morning plain, old, typical Turbo looked out on his plain, old, typical classroom in plain, old Sunnyview Elementary School. He smiled.

Earlier Ms. Beasley had arrived and found the pencil sharpener on her desk. Which had led her to look

at where the pencil sharpener was *supposed* to be, on the shelf above Turbo's cage. Which had led her to notice Turbo's cage. Which had led

her to realize that the pencil shavings from the pencil sharpener had
been falling *into* Turbo's cage!

Ms. Beasley had the janitor come

in and reinstall the pencil sharpener, this time on the corner of her
own desk.

RING-A-DING-DING!

"Okay, class," said Ms. Beasley when all the students were seated. "I have a few announcements this morning. First, I'm supposed to tell you that tomorrow we will be starting a trial in the cafeteria."

Turbo's ears perked up at the sound of this. Trial? Cafeteria?

"We're doing a trial run of great new snacks such as organic fruits and vegetables, gluten-free bread, hummus, and all kinds of yummy stuff," explained Ms. Beasley.

A boy in the back of the room raised his hand. "You're not getting rid of the old snacks too, are you?" he asked. "I'm on a very strict all-cheese diet."

Ms. Beasley laughed.
"No, Charlie," she told
the boy. "After this trial,

we'll be stocking the cafeteria with all sorts of delicious *and* healthy snacks."

At this, the class gave a cheer.

In his cage Turbo chuckled to himself. So *that* was the trial in the cafeteria! Mystery solved! Wait until he told the rest of the Superpet Superhero League!

Then Ms. Beasley told the students about how the pencil sharpener had been raining pencil shavings on poor Turbo, and how she'd had it reinstalled on her desk.

This time a different boy from the back of the room raised his hand. "Ms. Beasley, I feel really bad about making it rain pencil shavings on Turbo," he said. "Do you think we could all make it up to him by drawing pictures of him? That might show Turbo how special he is to us!"

"What a wonderful idea, Eugene!" Ms. Beasley exclaimed.

In his cage Turbo beamed.

At Ms. Beasley's desk the students lined up to sharpen their pencils.

For some reason, the sound wasn't so bad this time!

Then the kids spent the morning drawing pictures of their beloved classroom pet.

Hi TurBo!

sorry Turbo!

TURBo!

Turbo sat back in his cage, surrounded by all the beautiful drawings made for him by the students of
Classroom C.

It was certainly hard work being
the official pet of a second-grade
classroom, and even *more* work
being a superhero. But it sure was
worth it.

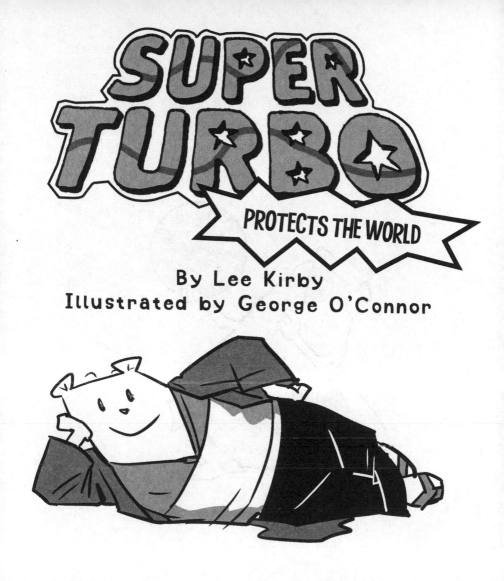

SUPER TURBO

PROTECTS THE WORLD

By Lee Kirby

Illustrated by George O'Connor

CONTENTS

IS IT HOT IN HERE?

BEHOLD! SUNNYVIEW ELEMENTARY SCHOOL! INSIDE THESE WALLS, UH . . .

Wait, where are we? Are we even inside the walls of Sunnyview Elementary School?

Turbo the hamster, official pet of Classroom C, lay on his belly. Sweat dripped from his furry forehead. Heat beat down from above, and even seemed to be rising from the ground itself. Around him, all Turbo could see was yellow sand.

Turbo squinted in the bright light. Wavy images seemed to appear from thin air. He saw a . . . slice of pizza? And a . . . monster truck? And a . . . giant dragon? Suddenly, there was a voice.

Turbo blinked. Could it be? Was it really who he thought it was? "Leo?"

Leo helped Turbo up from the rock he had been lying on. "Are you okay?" Leo asked. "You sat down and . . . I don't know . . . spaced out."

"Yeah," said Turbo, wiping his forehead with a paw. "It's really hot here."

WELL, I AM A GECKO. I LIKE IT HOT.

Turbo looked around. Now he remembered! He had been visiting his friend Leo in Classroom A. But while Turbo's home in Classroom C was a cozy cage filled with cedar chips and a water bottle, Leo's was a desert-like terrarium.

Leo was an official classroom pet. But like Turbo, Leo was not *just* a classroom pet. Turbo and Leo were both secretly superheroes!

But more on that later.

"Maybe we should get you a drink," said Leo.

Leo took Turbo to a small pool of water that looked like it had been carved out of rock. After a few gulps, Turbo felt much more like himself again.

"You have a really nice place, Leo," he said. "But I'm not sure it's quite right for me."

"I'll say." Leo laughed. "You fuzzy guys can't take the heat!"

Suddenly Leo leaped to his feet. "Did you hear that?"

TAP! TAP! TAP!

"It's the Superpet Superhero League alarm!" exclaimed Turbo. "And three taps means there's a super emergency!"

Wait, what's that you say? You've never heard of the Superpet Super- hero League?! Why, the Superpet Superhero League is only the best team of superpets in Sunnyview Elementary history!

Turbo and Leo quickly sprang into action. Within moments, they had transformed into . . .

2

FISH OUT OF WATER!

Super Turbo and the Great Gecko popped the cover off the vent in Classroom A. The vent system connected all the classrooms in Sunnyview Elementary.

The superpets listened closely to the sound of the taps.

Every member of the Superpet Superhero League used a different tool to tap for help. Turbo, for example, used a ruler. Since this pet was tapping with a pencil, that meant it was Clever!

Clever was a green parakeet, and she was the official pet of Classroom D. She was also a member of the Superpet Superhero League, where

she fought evil as the Green Winger.

Super Turbo followed the Great Gecko down the vent system leading to Classroom D. As they rounded a corner, they bumped into the other members of the Superpet Superhero League.

FRANK

ALIAS: BOSS BUNNY
CLASSROOM: PRINCIPAL'S OFFICE. YEAH, IT'S NOT REALLY A CLASSROOM. FRANK IS THE PERSONAL PET OF PRINCIPAL BAXTER BRICKFORD!
SUPERHERO SKILLS: HIS UTILITY BELT HAS A GADGET FOR ANY OCCASION! AND HE CAN SMELL DANGER!

WARREN

ALIAS: PROFESSOR TURTLE
CLASSROOM: THE SCIENCE LAB
SUPERHERO SKILLS: BEING A TURTLE, HE'S PRETTY SLOW, BUT HE'S ALSO SUPER SMART. ESPECIALLY WHEN IT COMES TO SCIENCE!

The Superpet Superhero League burst out of the vent that led into Classroom D. And there was the Green Winger, perched in her cage. As expected, she was frantic.

"Guys! Thank goodness you're here! Come quick!" she cried. She flew down to the floor of Classroom D and gestured for the other animals to follow her.

As Turbo scurried
along, he nearly
slipped in
something
slick.

"Why is
the floor
all wet?"
he asked.

"*That's* why!" the Green Winger said, and pointed at something flapping on the ground.

It was Nell!

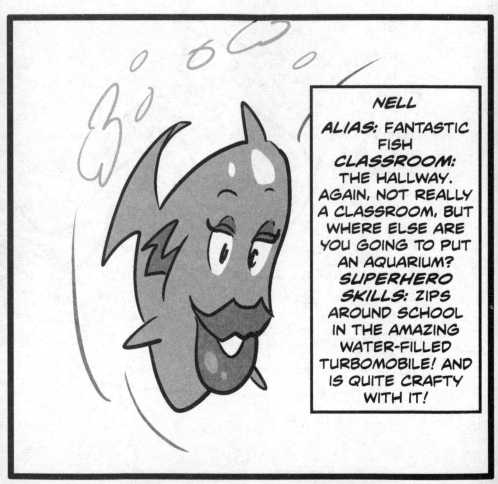

NELL

ALIAS: FANTASTIC FISH

CLASSROOM: THE HALLWAY. AGAIN, NOT REALLY A CLASSROOM, BUT WHERE ELSE ARE YOU GOING TO PUT AN AQUARIUM?

SUPERHERO SKILLS: ZIPS AROUND SCHOOL IN THE AMAZING WATER-FILLED TURBOMOBILE! AND IS QUITE CRAFTY WITH IT!

Nell lay on her side. Next to her was an almost-totally-empty Turbomobile.

"Hi, guys," Nell gasped. "A little help here?"

The Turbomobile had once been an ordinary hamster ball until the Superpet Superhero League had turned it into a way for Fantastic Fish to get around. It had allowed the fish to fight in many memorable battles with evil. But now it had apparently sprung a leak.

"Wonder Pig . . . ," began Professor Turtle. "Can you help me take the Turbomobile . . . to my lab? I want to . . . go over it and . . . fix any leaks."

"That's a great idea, Professor Turtle," said the Great Gecko. "With your scientific know-how, I'm sure you'll have the Turbomobile in better shape than ever! In the meantime, tomorrow is our regularly scheduled Superpet Superhero League meeting. Let's all get some well-earned rest before then."

"It *has* been a long night!" agreed Super Turbo.

And he meant it. As he headed back to Classroom C, he could barely keep his eyes open. Once he was in his cage, Turbo tucked away his superhero gear and fell fast asleep.

THE SUPERPET SUPERHERO LEAGUE GOES GLOBAL!

Turbo woke up early the next morning. He had slept deeply after his adventure in the desert—or, well, in Leo's terrarium—and after his hard work helping Nell.

RING-A-DING-DING!

The classroom bell! That meant school was starting. Since the students of Classroom C had no idea that their beloved class pet was actually a superhero, it was time for Turbo to act like a normal *non*-super hamster. The second-grade students and their teacher filed in.

Turbo ran a few laps on his wheel.

SQUEAK! SQUEAK! SQUEAK!

He ate a few hamster pellets.

He drank from his water bottle.

That should do it, thought Turbo, wiping his mouth with the back of his paw. Secret's still safe!

Ms. Beasley, the teacher, began to address the class. Turbo settled into his favorite listening spot next to his food dish. He used to pay no attention to what the teacher told the students of Classroom C, but Turbo had recently discovered that if he *did*

pay attention, he might actually learn something. As in: *learn* about *something* that might require a superhero to step in and save the day.

"Kids, I have exciting news," said Ms. Beasley. "For the next couple of weeks, the whole school is going to be participating in a very special project!"

Turbo's ears perked up. A special project sounded like superhero business.

"And that special project is . . . Celebrate the World Day!" Ms. Beasley announced.

"What's Celebrate the World Day?" asked a student.

"Good question, Sally," replied Ms. Beasley. "Leading up to the event, each class at Sunnyview Elementary will research and study one country. Then, the day of, the classes will celebrate the country they've studied! We'll decorate our classrooms, dress in traditional clothing, and serve traditional food. We'll travel around the world by going from class to class, and we'll learn all about different countries!"

Wow, thought Turbo. *That sounds pretty cool! Maybe we superpets don't need to step in after all.*

Ms. Beasley proceeded to announce which country each classroom would be celebrating.

Turbo listened excitedly. Wow!
The whole Superpet Superhero
league was involved. But something
was missing. There was one pet left

out. Turbo couldn't think of who it was. But then . . .

Hey, that's us! How exciting! thought Turbo. *But . . . where's Japan?*

Oh well, he'd have a lot of time to learn. Turbo couldn't wait until the pets' team meeting tonight so they could gush over this exciting new project. The Superpet Superhero League was going global!

Meanwhile, through a small crack in the wall near Classroom C's book nook, a pair of beady eyes were gleaming.

CELEBRATE THE WORLD DAY? MORE LIKE TAKE OVER THE WORLD DAY!

4

FUN FACTS AND RAT PACKS

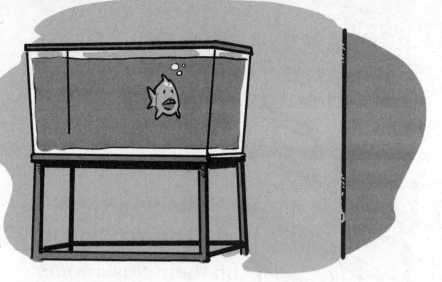

That night, all the animals were holding their Superpet Superhero League meeting in the hallway of Sunnyview Elementary. This way, Nell could attend. Professor Turtle was still working on fixing the Turbomobile.

On the way to the meeting, Turbo

and Angelina had stopped by the library to pick up some books, and the animals were eagerly reading up on their classrooms' countries.

The upcoming Celebrate the World Day was very exciting. So exciting, in fact, that the superpets had pretty much forgotten to be super. Instead they just traded cool facts about their countries with one another.

The superpets were so wrapped up in all these cool new facts that they didn't notice a couple of small fuzzy animals watching them from around the corner. The two animals whispered to each other and disappeared through a hole in the wall.

If the superpets *had* been paying attention, they might have seen these fuzzy creatures, followed them, and discovered that they went skittering through the walls, down the halls, and into the cafeteria, where they then joined a huge crowd of other fuzzy creatures. It was . . .

THE RAT PACK!

And in the middle of the pack, standing on a stale bagel, was . . .

WHISKERFACE!

Whiskerface was a tiny rat with huge ears who was just about as evil as they come.

"I need a report on our plans for sabotage!" he bellowed. "Starting with Classroom A!"

Two rats stepped forward. "The kindergarteners of Classroom A will be celebrating Brazil," said one of them. "The most popular sport in Brazil is soccer."

"*Futbol*," corrected the other rat. "They call it *futbol*."

"Yeah, yeah. They're building a miniature *futbol* stadium. We're going to chew through the supports of their tiny stands, and smash it all with a soccer ball attack!"

"Excellent!" said Whiskerface, rubbing his little paws together. "Classroom B! Report!"

Two more rats came forward. "The first-grade students of Classroom B are making their own Leaning Tower of Pisa," said one rat. "We're going to make sure the leaning tower leans over a liiiiiittle too far!"

"Then it will fall, smashing the classroom as flat

as a pizza!" said the other.

Whiskerface laughed his squeaky high-pitched laugh. "Classroom C!"

"The highest point in Japan is Mount Fuji. It's a volcano! The students are making a model," said a rat.

"We're going to make that volcano erupt!" cried his companion nastily.

"Yes! Yes!" shouted Whiskerface, clapping. "Classroom D!"

"Classroom D is Kenya!" another rat announced. "The Third graders are making giant models of safari animals. We will sneak our agents *into* the giraffe model. Bet those kids didn't think a cardboard giraffe could actually walk!"

Whiskerface cackled with delight. "What else do we have?"

"The science lab is going to be Switzerland. They are recreating Lake Geneva. And we're going to make sure that lake overflows!"

"The principal's office will be Russia. They're going to be making borscht." The rat who spoke shuddered with disgust. "Borscht is a cold beet soup. And it's gross. So we kind of figure that's already ruined," he said.

"And, finally," said one rat, as he walked forward, "the hallways are China. In ancient times, China was connected to the rest of the world by trade routes called the Silk Road. The students are turning the hallways into a modern Silk Road."

"But!" said another rat, smiling. "We're going to block the hallways with our very own Great Wall of China! Everyone will be trapped in their classrooms!"

5

NIGHTTIME NOISES

Turbo was snug as a bug in his hamster cage when he heard it. He wasn't sure what it was, but he knew it was *something*. The last time Turbo woke up to a strange sound in the middle of the night, he ended up having to battle the evil Pencil Pointer.

He listened as hard as he could with his little hamster ears. He thought he could make out the sound of . . . squeaking?

"Hello? Is anyone there?" Turbo called out.

The squeaking stopped. Well, that was suspicious.

SURELY THIS IS A JOB FOR . . . SUPER TURBO!

Using his super-hamster agility, Super Turbo snuck out of his cage and quietly scampered across the classroom to Ms. Beasley's desk. That's where the squeaking seemed to be coming from.

Super Turbo discovered that the bottom desk drawer was wide open. Then he looked up and saw that the other desk drawers had been opened, too, but only partway.

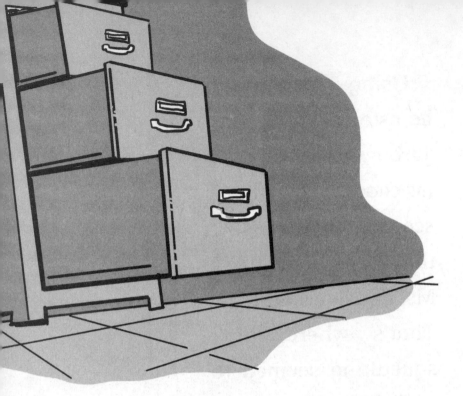

Looks oddly like a staircase,
Super Turbo thought. *And what
would Super Turbo do? He'd climb
that staircase!*

The only problem was . . . even
Super Turbo was still pretty small.

He took a running start and . . .
SMACK! He bounced off the bottom
drawer.

That was all the boost he needed. Super Turbo climbed up the drawer-stairs to the top of Ms. Beasley's desk and was face-to-face with . . . no one.

Whoever had opened the drawers, whoever had been here, whoever had been *squeaking*, had left.

From where he now stood on top of Ms. Beasley's desk, Super Turbo realized that he had a perfect view of the whole class and all its decorations!

Super Turbo admired all the hard work the kids of Classroom C had put into Celebrate the World Day. More than ever, he felt that he needed to keep a watchful eye over the classroom.

Suddenly, he heard another noise. But this time, it was different.

The Superpet Superhero Alarm! But which superpet was tapping?

TAP! TAP! TAP!

Super Turbo concentrated. The taps were sort of hard and sort of waxy? It was a crayon! That meant he needed to get to Classroom A immediately! The Great Gecko was in trouble!

AROUND THE WORLD IN TWENTY MINUTES

All of the superpets had gathered in
Classroom A, except for Fantastic
Fish, who was still stuck in her tank.

"Just putting a few touches on the
Turbomobile," explained Professor
Turtle.

The animals were huddled around
the Great Gecko, who was staring

at a giant piece of paper that lay on the floor. It was slightly torn and a little crumpled.

"Just look at it!" he said sadly. "It's ruined!'

BRAZIL

"I'll say!" said Boss Bunny. "It looks like it was painted by a bunch of five-year-olds."

"That's because it *was* painted by a bunch of five-year-olds!" cried the Great Gecko. "This was the banner my kids made to celebrate their country, Brazil! They worked so hard on it. And now it's destroyed!"

"Uh, guys," said Wonder Pig. "If Whiskerface and his Rat Pack are still out there. And we're all in here—"

"Then who's protecting our classrooms?!" cried the Green Winger.

"I think . . . it will be faster . . . if we split up . . . and each go to . . . our own rooms," said Professor Turtle, as quickly as he possibly could. He looked around. The other superpets had already run off. "Oh . . . never mind, then."

The superpets raced through the vents and arrived at Classroom B, Wonder Pig's home.

"Oh no!" Wonder Pig shouted. "The Leaning Tower of

Pisa looks like it's leaning a liiiittle too much!"

Boss Bunny sniffed the air. "I think they've already left! Let's go to the next class!"

The superpets ran to Classroom D, home base of the Green Winger. Just as they arrived, a loud *CRASH* rang out.

"Oh no!" exclaimed the Green Winger. "They just spilled these beads all over the floor! My kids had been sorting these for days!"

The superpets ran back to the vent and hurried to the science lab. They arrived seconds after Professor Turtle, who had gone straight there at his usual turtle speed. Everything was covered in what looked like snow!

Boss Bunny sniffed the air. "It smells so clean!" he cried with delight.

"That's because . . . these are flakes of . . . *soap*," concluded Professor Turtle. "It's a . . . soapy avalanche!" he said, looking around in horror.

Once again, the superpets were already racing out the door.

"Superpets!" shouted Nell from her aquarium in the hallway. "I just saw them! They ran under the door to the principal's office! If you hurry, you can catch them!"

That did it for Boss Bunny.

No one messed with Principal Brickford's office!

With a mighty bunny hop, Boss Bunny hurled himself at the mail slot in the door of the principal's office.

And the superpets did hurry, but by the time they got the door open, the Rat Pack was long gone.

Fortunately, it looked like they hadn't done any damage there.

But they sure had done a lot to the rest of the school. And it was up to the superpets to fix this mess before the students and teachers arrived the next morning.

It was going to be a long, long night.

7

TODAY'S THE DAY!

It had taken the superpets all night
and even into the early morning to
clean up the ugly worldwide mess.
Then they had spent the rest of the
week looking for the Rat Pack in
the cafeteria, but Whiskerface and
his evil minions were nowhere to be
found.

Turbo was in his cage in Classroom C, pacing back and forth. Today was the big one. Today was Celebrate the World Day. If the Rat Pack was going to pull some dirty move, it was going to happen *now*.

Turbo was sure that they were planning something *truly* evil.

Suddenly Turbo noticed that one of his students was staring at him. Pacing back and forth wasn't exactly normal hamster behavior, so he

quickly ran over to his hamster wheel and began running on it.

To be fair, Turbo wasn't looking very *normal* right now anyway.

As part of Celebrate the World Day, some students had dressed Turbo in a hamster-sized traditional Japanese outfit. Turbo thought it looked pretty cool, though it didn't really leave room for his cape.

Turbo glanced at the clock. Soon, the students of Classroom C, along with the rest of Sunnyview Elementary, would head to the school cafeteria. That was where they were having the great feast with food from around the world.

The Superpet Superhero League had decided that as soon as all the kids left their classrooms, the pets would gather for an emergency meeting.

It was risky business. They had never met during school hours before, but they had never faced such a threat before either! Whatever Whiskerface and his Rat Pack were up to, they had to be stopped!

And the Superpet Superhero League was the school's only defense.

RING-A-DING-DING!

The lunch bell rang, and the students of Classroom C filed out of the classroom. Turbo slipped from his cage, crawled down the table, and made his way to the vent. He managed to awkwardly tuck his cape into his kimono.

He scurried through the vents to the meeting place: below the aquarium in the hallway. When Super Turbo arrived, he gasped.

WOW, LOOK AT YOU GUYS!

Suddenly, a squeaky voice rang out behind the superpets. "Well, I think you look like a bunch of ninnies!"

It was Whiskerface! And his Rat Pack!

PROTECTING THE SCHOOL—AND THE WORLD!

Whiskerface paced back and forth, gleefully rubbing his paws together. "Do you know why today is a great day? Not only am I going to defeat the superpests—I'm going to ruin Celebrate the World Day, and then I'm going to take over the *actual* world!" he cackled.

"We're *not* going to let you ruin Celebrate the World Day!" cried Turbo.

"Oh really?" said Whiskerface with a sneer. "Well, guess what? You're too late!"

Whiskerface snapped his fingers. On cue, the Rat Pack swarmed the hallway. They linked arms to form a rather disgusting-looking chain of rats, completely blocking the hall.

The Rat Pack advanced on the superpets. On the other side of the wall, Turbo saw that a second group of rats was creating a tower by standing on top of one another so that they could lock the cafeteria door. If they reached that lock, they really *would* trap the entire school!

"We've got to stop them!" cried Turbo. But how?!

Suddenly, a loud rumbling sound filled the hallway.

"I *still* say you left a few steps out of that plan of yours!" yelled Fantastic Fish. She was in the new-and-improved Turbomobile. And riding on top was Boss Bunny!

9

THE FANTASTICALLY FISHY PLAN!

The Fantastic Fish Tank burst through the great wall of rats, scattering them like bowling pins. Boss Bunny hopped off the back, joining his friends.

"Sorry we're late," he apologized.

"Actually, I'd say you guys were right on time!" cried Super Turbo.

Meanwhile, Fantastic Fish spun down the hallway in her Fantastic Fish Tank. She smacked into the tower of rats.

"What are you doing?!" screamed Whiskerface to his Rat Pack. All the rats were walking around a bit dazed. "Get that talking fish!" he shrieked.

But Fantastic Fish was a few steps ahead of the evil rat. She steered the Fantastic Fish Tank at full speed right for her aquarium.

The Superpet Superhero League stared at her, afraid of what was about to happen.

At the last second, Fantastic Fish unlatched the top of the Fantastic Fish Tank. Then she leaped out. And just in the nick time!

Whiskerface and the Rat Packers were soaked. If there's anything rats hate more than loud noises and superpets, it's being wet. Crying like babies, Whiskerface and his Rat Pack scampered down the hallway.

The superpets ran over to Fantastic Fish, who lay flopping in a shallow puddle.

"Oh no!" cried the Green Winger.
"Not again!"

"Get back to your classrooms,"
gasped Fantastic Fish. "Turbo, hide
the new Fantastic Fish Tank. Oh, I
also renamed the Turbomobile. Is
that okay?"

"Of course it is!" said Super Turbo.
"But we can't leave you here!"

"Listen, I'll be fine," Fantastic Fish said. "With the commotion we created, people are going to come running. Any second now, someone will help me."

"Now, that's what I call a hero!" said the Great Gecko.

"Guys . . . we've got . . . to go. I hear someone . . . coming," said Professor Turtle.

The rest of the superpets heard it too. With a last glance at Fantastic Fish, Super Turbo and the others raced away just as Ms. Beasley and a crowd of students burst from the cafeteria.

10

SAFE AND SOUND

A little while later, Turbo sat in his comfy cage, munching on some seaweed and edamame. What a day it had been! The Superpet Superhero League had faced perhaps their greatest challenge yet, and they had won! And to top it off, they had even kept their secret identities safe.

Turbo turned to look at the glass
jar next to him on the shelf.

"Care for some edamame?" he
asked Nell.

After the commotion in the hallway, Ms. Beasley had been the first
to find Nell. She'd taken Nell back
to Classroom C and put her safely

inside a jar of water, just until her aquarium could be replaced.

"No, thanks," Nell replied. "I'm more of a dried worm kind of gal."

The students of Classroom C were busy presenting all they knew about Japan to students from other classes.

They would never know how close
Celebrate the World Day had come
to being ruined, but that didn't matter. Turbo was just glad that Whiskerface had been stopped . . . this time.
Surely there would be another time

when the school—and the world—
needed protecting. And when that
time came . . .

THE SUPERPET SUPERHERO LEAGUE
WOULD BE THERE!

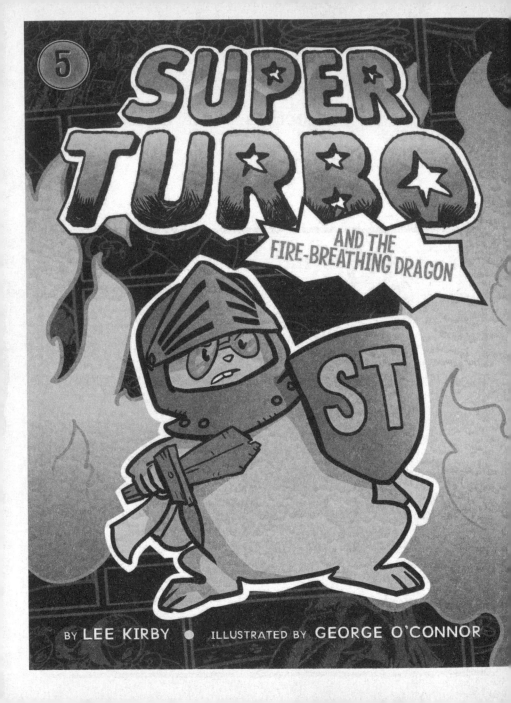

Can you keep a secret? Yes? Great. We'll come back to that. At the moment, that sure is one sad hamster who's moping in his cage. A hamster named Turbo.

Turbo hasn't eaten since yesterday. He doesn't even have the energy to jog on his hamster wheel. And while he normally loves keeping a watchful eye on Classroom C—that's his duty as the official class pet—today he doesn't even feel like doing that.

Why, you might wonder?

Well, it all began with an evil rat named Whiskerface. Whiskerface's main goal in life was to try to take over the world. Recently, he had tried to test out that plan right here at Sunnyview Elementary. But what he didn't expect was to have to face the Superpet Superhero League.

That brings us back to the big secret. You see, Turbo the hamster isn't your ordinary hamster. He's actually . . . Super Turbo!

And he's a member of the Superpet Superhero League! The league is made up of all the class pets at Sunnview Elementary. Together, these superheroic pets have one mission: making sure the school is kept safe. And often this means battling evil like Whiskerface, flying ninja squirrels, and villains like the Pencil Pointer.

When Whiskerface tried to test out his world-takeover, the Superpet Superhero League had stood in his way!

But during the battle, Nell—also known as Fantastic Fish—had lost her home. She usually lived in a large aquarium in the hallway. That aquarium had shattered on the floor during the fight, so she'd spent the last week in *Turbo's* classroom, right next to his hamster cage! They had been having the best time.

Then, just yesterday, someone had come to take Nell away. It turned out they'd gotten her a brand-new state-of-the-art aquarium. Turbo knew he should be happy for Nell, but truthfully, he was sad to see her go.

Turbo was feeling pretty sorry for himself, when suddenly the school bell rang. His kids! He had lost track of time. It was the start of the school day, which meant all the students of Ms. Beasley's second-grade class would be entering the classroom soon. They always cheered him up. The kids loved Turbo and often did drawings of him or brought him little treats. Today, one of his favorite students, a boy named Eugene McGillicudy, showed Turbo a drawing he'd done of himself as a superhero named Captain Awesome.

Turbo made little hamster noises of approval. After all, he couldn't actually tell Eugene how much he liked the drawing. That would give away his supersecret!

The day went by surprisingly quickly despite the fact that Turbo didn't have his friend Nell next to him. Soon enough, the last school bell rang and the kids filed out of the classroom.

As soon as the school lights were off, Turbo climbed out of his cage and scampered down to the reading nook of Classroom C. That was where the Superpet Superhero League had their supersecret meetings, and it was time for today's!

Angelina, also known as Wonder Pig, was the first to arrive. The cover of the vent in Classroom C popped off and out she crawled.

That was how the Superpets got around the school—through the vent system! It was also how they communicated with one another. If there was ever trouble, a pet would tap something on the inside of the vent and the sound would echo throughout all the vents, alerting the rest of the pets to come quickly!

Angelina was followed by Leo,

also known as the Great Gecko, who came crawling out of the vent with Clever, also known as the Green Winger. Frank, also known as Boss Bunny, came next. He was with Nell!

Finally, slow as ever, came Warren. His superhero name was Professor Turtle.

With the Superpet Superhero League all there, the meeting could begin.

"First order of business," said Leo, who often ran the meetings. "Happy birthday, Angelina!"

Angelina blushed. "Thanks, Leo," she said.

Turbo didn't know it was Angelina's birthday! It wasn't that long ago that he'd even discovered there were other class pets, so he was still getting to know all of them.

"After we're done with our meeting, we'll all head to the cafeteria for a special treat," said Leo. "So, who has something to report?"

"Well, you guys have to come check out my new aquarium sometime," said Nell. "I now have five different types of coral. Five! And there's this awesome cave that I use as my top-secret headquarters."

All the superpets thought that sounded pretty cool.

"I perfected a new trick," said Clever. Being a bird, she was really acrobatic.

The rest of the pets clapped and cheered as Clever performed her impressive trick. When she landed, she bowed.

"I . . . have . . . some . . . news," began Warren.

The rest of the pets waited patiently for Warren to reveal the news. And when he did, they were more curious than ever. Warren told them that the science teacher, Dr. Garfield, had announced to his last class of the day that when they came back for science the next afternoon, there would be a surprise in the classroom.

As the pets headed to the cafeteria, they took turns guessing what the surprise might be.

"Nell's being moved back to my classroom?" Turbo suggested hopefully. But even he knew that was a long shot.

"They're installing a roller coaster on the playground?" Nell offered.

"We get to eat human food all the time?!" Frank shouted.

"Not likely," said Leo. "But speaking of human food . . ." Leo trailed off as he gestured toward something that was on the floor in the middle of the cafeteria.

It was a half-eaten, slightly smushed cake with a candle in it.

"Isn't it beautiful?" said Leo proudly. "Frank and Clever helped me transport it from the teacher's lounge, and we even found a candle in the garbage!"

Angelina was beaming. "It's perfect,"she told her friends."Let's dig in!"

But Turbo was too distracted to eat at the moment. Warren had said there was going to be a surprise in the science lab. Sometimes surprises were good. But sometimes . . . they were evil.

The next morning, Turbo woke up especially early. He was still thinking about that surprise. And he hoped that whatever it was, Warren was okay.

Turbo thought about it all morning. While the kids in the classroom were taking a spelling test, he even considered trying to sneak out.

But he decided it was too risky. So Turbo waited for the day to end. He waited . . . and waited. And finally, the classroom emptied out.

I've got to go check on Warren, Turbo thought.

LEE KIRBY has the proportionate strength and abilities of a man-size hamster. He spends his days chewing up cardboard and running in giant plastic bubbles throughout his very own fortress of solitude in Brooklyn, New York. And, no, he is not related to world-famous Captain Awesome author Stan Kirby. Or is he?

GEORGE O'CONNOR is the creator of the *New York Times* bestselling graphic novel series Olympians, in addition to serving as the illustrator of the Captain Awesome series. He is also the author and illustrator of the picture books *Kapow!*, *Ker-splash*, and *If I Had a Triceratops*. He resides in his secret Brooklyn, New York, hideout, where he uses his amazing artistic powers to strike fear in the hearts of bad guys everywhere!